I0670621

Totally Bound Publishing books by Katherine McIntyre

Tribal Spirits

FORGED DECISIONS

KATHERINE MCINTYRE

Forged Decisions
ISBN # 978-1-913186-17-3
©Copyright Katherine McIntyre 2019
Cover Art by Erin Dameron-Hill ©Copyright January 2019
Interior text design by Claire Siemaszkiewicz
Totally Bound Publishing

FORGED
DECISIONS

Dedication

To family, both blood and not, who prove that
time and distance don't change the unbreakable
bonds we've forged.

Chapter One

Finn had been avoiding Beaver Tavern all week.

He sat in his Challenger, tapping ash out of the window as he stared down Raven's car in the parking lot. Sneaking around, hiding from her at every chance — he was being pure chickenshit right now. The Tavern had already flicked on the open sign for the day and ever since the night of Dax's victory when he'd spent the night with Navi, he hadn't wanted to face Raven. Hadn't wanted to untangle the complicated whatever they'd been dancing around all these years. His wolf lunged inside him, demanding straightforwardness he couldn't muster right now.

He let out a stream of smoke, glancing at the time on his car's interface. With his next class in a half-hour, he didn't have long enough to dive into a serious conversation with her. His throat tightened when he wheeled the car out of the lot and his tires crunched over gravel. Even as he made the justifications in his mind, he knew he hid behind excuse after excuse.

A better man would've never strung Raven along this long, knowing at the end of the day they would never have a future together.

Finn wasn't a better man — hell, he wasn't even a good man most days. The previous alpha had groomed Sierra to take the reins and not him for a reason, despite their matched skills and strength. The current alpha of the Red Rock pack maintained the unshakable moral code his people needed to hold their territory and form a united front against any challengers that might come their way. Finn threw out a whole lot of swagger, but time and time again, he crumbled.

The hickory and oak trees of Rickett's Glen rolled by, the dense forests he'd grown up running through. Those trails beckoned to his wolf on a regular basis since he skated a little more on the wild than the others, a little too attuned to the demands of his other side. He drove this route to work daily on the way to his studio. Thank everything holy he'd carved a successful niche teaching kickboxing and MMA out here, because if he hadn't found some outlet for his aggression, he'd be flipping tables and slinging punches every night.

After the way he'd wussed out of the discussion with Raven yet again, he needed to burn some of the nerves making him buzz. Which made the upcoming class he was teaching perfect timing.

He pulled up in front of his studio, Kelly's Gym, and parked along the patch of beaten earth that constituted the parking lot. Finn approached the shoebox of a place he couldn't have been prouder of, the plaster siding glowing white and the near-flat black roof within jumping distance. His place might not compare to the massive gyms in cities like Philly, but he'd thrown a lot of work over the years into turning what used to be a couple of sessions a week into a thriving business.

He loped up the steps and unlocked the door, the light stuttering on once he flipped the switch. The pale white walls of his gym interior needed a new paint job, since every imperfection glared brighter against the red and black mats lining the floor and the six drop-down punching bags. The sets of weights lining the back were stacked neatly in place—folks might call him anal retentive, but he shouldered a fair amount of personal pride in this place, which he wanted to represent as a clean, organized space.

Finn strode to the back and set the big fans on, his sole means to combat the sticky heat rolling through this sector during late summer. Once strong breezes gusted through the room, he began his own set of warm-ups, his wolf snapping at the reins a little more than normal. Not like he thought he'd be less agitated in charge—Sierra made an amazing alpha—but ever since he'd become beta of the pack, a restlessness had kept him on edge.

Even with their old alpha, his wolf had lunged forward to strike at any chance, a rebellious side of him that clashed with the community he needed to survive. Wolves were pack creatures and he'd witnessed life outside their circle early on when his shithead folks decided to ditch. The time away had been a nightmare.

Drops of sweat beaded Finn's brow as he worked his reps with the punching bag, burning some of the aggression heating his chest. One-two, one-two, one-two.

A slight creak from the opposite side of the room startled the hell out of him. Finn whipped around, droplets flying from his arms when he turned toward the door he'd never heard open.

"Don't stop for my sake—I was enjoying the show," Navi drawled, leaning against one of the pillars in the center of the room. The damn panther could sneak around better than most, even with the raw, lethal energy radiating from her. Like Finn needed more of a knockout punch — the sight of her shoved the air from him. Navi's hooded gaze, those deep hazel eyes screamed sex, and the casual smirk on her full lips was a private one she'd only shared since the other night.

The tank top and running shorts she wore left her rich brown skin on full display, highlighting the sort of hips he wouldn't have expected on a pipsqueak like her. Not that he'd ever call her that — he might be a dumbass sometimes, but he valued his life. She was one of the Tribe, the shifters imbued with the great spirits of the animals they transformed into and the governing force of their kind.

When he'd started flirting with the scary-as-fuck Tribe member during Dax's trials, he knew he was playing with fire, but he expected her to shut him down. Never in a thousand years had he anticipated their unforgettable night.

Man and wolf alike couldn't help the way his cock throbbed at the mere sight of her. When she moved, he noticed, and when she entered a room, he felt her presence as loudly as if she screamed in his ear.

"Got some aggression to burn before class, soldier?" she asked, approaching with a balanced, feline grace to her movements. His heartbeat raced. He wanted to slam her against the mats to claim every inch of her luscious body, but she patted the side of the punching bag. "We've tried that route," she purred, her eyes glinting with amusement. "Now let's see how you fight."

Inches separated them and Finn stepped closer, moving into her space. "How's that a fair fight, pussycat? You've got all those spirit-gifted tricks to whip out."

Navi didn't back down an inch, her calm smile twisting into a smirk. "Like I need my abilities to bring you to your knees. Quit making excuses, Finn Kelly, and spar with me."

His heart thumped in his ears, the blood pumping through his veins in an intoxicating way. A slow grin rolled onto his face as he stepped back a pace and sank into a crouch. "I suppose we've got enough time for one round. Don't go crying to your buddies that a Red Rock kicked your ass."

Her mouth quirked with her grin, but Navi emanated lethal calm, her eyes flashing the silver of her panther even though she remained in human form. She was out of his league in every way, her abilities and the magic at her command the stuff of whispered legends, and yet Finn couldn't help trying to catch the tornado by the tail. As she circled around him, the movement slow and seductive, her power crashed down like a tidal wave over the room until Finn near drowned in it.

Too bad he was a stubborn fucker.

He bared his teeth, fangs forming while he watched her with a wolf's vigilance. A cat like her could play and tease forever—he knew without a doubt between the two of them, she'd hold out longer. He rolled his shoulders, the urge to lash out prickling through him. Thankfully, he'd never refined an attack style relying on patience. Finn had been throwing punches before he ever learned to speak, and teaching for a long time — long enough to see a thousand types of styles and figure out how to combat them.

She watched his every movement, waiting for him to tip off his first strike—which meant he needed to employ either speed, or a feint.

Maybe both.

Finn tilted his right shoulder forward to test the waters and tossed a few one-two punches in her direction. Navi's palm blocked one and her forearm deflected the other.

Would she take the bait?

The micro-second twitch of her knee gave him the hint.

Right when she tried to thrust her knee into the opening, Finn pivoted out of the way. He grabbed her closest arm and tugged, throwing her hips off balance, and before she could right herself, he stepped in close and personal. With the opposite forearm, he slammed into her stomach. To his surprise, she didn't stumble, just toed a few paces in the sort of dance anyone skilled enough could muster.

Inches away, he didn't stand a chance of avoiding her punch.

The blow slammed into his stomach, and only the quickstep away helped diminish the force. This close, he could smell the vanilla scent of her skin, could see the way her forearms tensed into corded muscle, honed for lethality like his own. Her gaze flashed, giving him the one heads-up of where she would move to next.

Her hips pivoted as she unleashed a kick.

Instead of running, Finn surged forward, square in the center where the knee hit. Before her leg thudded against his body, he'd already tackled her. Navi wouldn't appreciate him holding back and he'd learned to use his muscle and heft to his advantage. Even as her thighs tensed and she tried to shove him, he sank like a stone overtop her. Together, they crashed to the ground.

He landed on top with his forearm pressed over her chest. She tilted her hip to the side, but he refused to move his weight. "Check," he said, a grin stealing his lips as her eyes blazed.

Her leg slipped between his thighs a second later. The moment he felt the movement coming, he rolled to the side. If she nailed him in the nuts, he'd be incapacitated.

Navi pounced, taking the foreground when she tackled him. The elbow she drove into his chest stung like a motherfucker, but he couldn't help the smile that appeared on his face. The dogged persistence she fought him with reminded him of his bouts with Sierra and the way Navi analyzed on the fly never failed to impress him. She was the sort of fight that wasn't just about proving something—right now, they were having fun.

He shoved her off again and she rolled into a crouch, rising at the same time as him. Her wicked grin mirrored his own as her shoulders heaved up and down from their form of play. She circled again, a predatory spark in her eyes. Finn's heart raced, sweat trickling down his forehead. Hell on earth, he was so alive while he tracked her movements, ready to dive in again.

"Getting tired already?" he taunted, rolling his shoulders as he prepared for another lunge.

"Tired of listening to you jaw off, Kelly," she retorted, even though her eyes sparked with amusement.

This time she took the initiative.

Her sneaker ground against the floor with a squeak when she launched through the air toward him. His instinct begged him to throw his hands out and catch her, following with another tackle—but instincts lied and she was clever.

Instead of lashing out, Navi tilted her right shoulder forward, making no effort to guard her body.

Finn barely got his arms up in defense as she slammed into him full force, using her body like a bludgeoning weapon. Despite her small size, she grounded herself like a powerhouse. Finn staggered back, the blow throwing him off kilter.

Except she didn't stop there.

Navi lashed out with her fists, needling two quick jabs into his open spots.

Instead of falling back or losing his balance, Finn danced on his feet since he kept his body loose to absorb the blows. They stung something fierce, but Navi wasn't throwing her full weight into them. Which meant she was planning something else. Her hip twitched to the right.

Finn thrust his arms down. The moment her leg snapped out, his hands wrapped around it. The side-sweep she attempted halted when he used his steadied stance to shove her leg out. Before she could regain her position, he pushed her forward, sending her tipping back. Finn's heart pounded, a grin stole over his face and sweat trickled down his neck, his shoulders. He leapt forward to tackle her to the ground.

She threw a jab straight to his gut, enough to make his stomach squeeze. However, he refused to relent and crashed onto her with his full weight. They tumbled to the ground again.

Her chest pulsed beneath him, her sweat-slicked limbs tangled with his. Their eyes met, a wild wickedness in Navi's that sent his mind to dirty, dirty places, reminding him of all the other things he'd like to do to her pinned to these mats.

The door to his studio creaked, drawing his attention at once.

"Am I interrupting something?" Kyle asked. The Silver Springs shifter scratched the back of his neck while he tried to avert his stare.

Finn hopped off Navi, but before he could offer a hand up, she rolled to her feet.

"Just your trainer getting his ass thrashed," she called as she made her way to the far wall lined with towels. She wiped away the thick strands of her pixie cut that had plastered to her forehead. He followed her over there, already covered in a sticky film of sweat he wanted to shower off, a combination of exertion and the August heat spreading through this place.

Finn snorted. "Kyle, get started on your basic stretches — we'll get rolling in a minute."

"Want to walk me to my car?" Navi asked, phrasing it less as a question and more as a demand. While the woman possessed a confident sexiness, she didn't do subtle for shit. Honestly, he liked that about her at once — Finn had been on the receiving end of so many mixed messages and sent some of his own, enough that he wanted a clean break from that sort of mess.

"Sure thing, sweetheart," he said, slinging his towel around his neck. Her eyebrows lifted at the term, one Sierra would've smacked him in the face for, but, for some reason, every time he pushed with Navi, she tolerated his cocky bullshit. Like she could see right through every ounce of bravado he flung her way. The mats squished under his tread while Finn and Navi made their way across his gym, out into the blazing heat.

When he stepped under the glaring sun, his skin heated in response, begging to soak in the rays and turn his olive skin three shades darker. Navi's old Plymouth sat out in the parking lot, the paint peeling and more than a couple of dents on the exterior. Finn's fingers itched to grab his toolkit and fix the sedan as best he could. Sierra had once told him he 'mother henned' over his Challenger with the amount of attention he poured into keeping his girl running smoothly.

"So, I'm guessing you didn't show up to tangle around on the mats with me," he said, leaning against her car, the metallic body creaking from his weight.

"Color me surprised, Sherlock," she drawled. "Didn't think you had a brain behind the pretty face." She leaned against the car beside him, her proximity comfortable.

"To be fair, you're as blunt as a sledgehammer," he responded, tugging at his wifebeater, which had glued to his chest.

"I'm not familiar with this area, and I'm going to need help from someone who knows every inch of this terrain. Sierra recommended you, but I needed to get a grip on your fighting style, because what I'm going to ask you isn't short on danger." Navi gave him a serious look that was all Tribe, pride and regality emanating from her. So different from the expressive woman who'd melted for him in the bedroom.

His skin prickled at the idea of danger and his wolf pounded approval in his chest. He'd been straining at the seams following orders here—even the normal responsibilities didn't appeal to him since he'd seen Sierra inundated with resolving the stupidest conflicts, and as her beta, he wasn't needed for much. He wanted to be in the thick of doing something useful and had honed his body into a weapon begging to be aimed and used.

"Sign me up," he responded, his tone firm.

Navi crossed her arms over her chest. "Don't even want to know what we're up against?"

Finn shrugged. "I trust you're not going to throw me into a suicide mission—you think I've got a pretty face." Navi's gaze bored into him at the comment, but those full lips quirked with a smile. When he'd first met the hardass, intimidating Tribe member, he never would've thought she had a sense of humor or even that theirs aligned.

"According to the supplier of those pipe bombs planted at the Silver Springs houses, the Landsliders are involved—the reason we came into town. You'll be helping us track down their outposts, which means I'm going to brief you on information about the man we're tracking, intel you've got to keep to yourself. Sierra's given us the necessary permissions, because you won't be able to share this with your pack." Navi watched him with an intensity that made his blood burn. As if she was testing him this very moment to see if he'd jump or run the other way.

What she didn't know is he'd been waiting for a chance, waiting for some way to unleash and let his wolf run free for far too long. This sort of fight, against an unknown, powerful enemy—this was something he could throw his whole heart and soul into.

Finn flashed her a grin, his teeth sharpening at the edges. "You had me at danger."

Chapter Two

The scent of moldering fabric and a too-floral fragrance that belonged in a nursing home greeted Navi upon entering the Dusty Pines Hotel. The Tribe's current base of operations looked like an eighty-year-old spinster had taken to decorating, which did little to add to any menacing vibe. However, the bitch about being impartial amongst packs meant they lived a life of constant hotel-hops, since staying in a pack residence might be construed as favoritism. Between the faded rose curtains and the cross-stitch of cats displayed on the wall of this place, Navi was pretty certain she'd stepped into a side dimension of hell.

Sweat had dried on her skin from getting physical with Finn Kelly, something she never should've done the first night. Those umber eyes had spelled trouble the moment she'd first locked gazes with him and ever since then she hadn't be able to get the cocky bastard off her mind. Navi brushed a few sticky strands of hair from her forehead as she sauntered across the rumpled carpeting to the room she and Jess shared. With her crew taking a couple of rooms in this joint for an indefinite time, she could guarantee they were making the Dusty Pines' sales for a year.

Navi Tremere had one rule. No attachments.

Not because she was some freak incapable of emotions, or a commitment-phobe—hell, she would give anything to settle down with the right guy—but that sort of future was never in her cards. Navi had been born as one of the Tribe, and she would carry that life sentence for the rest of her days. Out of her circle, only Akio had managed to nab a wife, and Navi witnessed firsthand the strain he went through when they got assigned to quell a pack war and she ended up in a hot zone. When that many shifters fought, even the Tribe struggled to handle them and they were equipped with supercharged abilities.

On one hand, the powers the shamans had imbued into her through the tattoos along her arms to her legs gave her abilities most shifters dreamed of. Navi could summon water at will to unleash it in a blast and she could compel shifters to follow orders, an ability she didn't take lightly. On the other hand, her life belonged to the Tribe. To traveling the East Coast as the ruling force amongst the shifters.

She didn't bother knocking—she and Jess had long thrown away the concept of privacy—and strolled into the room. Without a word of greeting, Navi flopped onto the bed and buried her face in the musty blankets. Now she'd be working in close proximity for who knew how long with Finn and those muscles she wanted to bite. With the golden undertones in his skin, the boy had a good amount of color on him for a white guy. Her panther purred every time she walked into his vicinity, a literal cat call roaring inside.

"You reek," Jess called from where she'd set up on the other bed, her laptop illuminating her skin and the tousled strands of hair that slipped from her braid. "Like a cloud of BO and sweat, babe. Why don't you hit the shower?"

"Because I enjoy annoying you," Navi shot back, sliding up on the bed to clutch the pillow tight. "What's the update on the Landslider activity?"

"You recruit some help?" Jess asked, glancing her way from the computer's embrace. "I've got a town a few miles up that needs some investigating. Word on the country backroad is they've been trafficking their wares via Ye Olde General Store."

"What sort of hillbilly hell have we descended into?" Navi groaned into her pillow. "We spent longer than necessary playing referee for the Silver Springs pack debacle, which interfered with making headway on our number one priority—the Landsliders." As much as she complained, her time here hadn't all been bad. The night after Dax's victory when Finn had had the balls to flirt with her while the rest of the pack guys veered away in fear—well, she'd be remembering the mind-blowing sex for a long time to come.

"I'm sure in a couple of weeks we'll be on to the next spot," Jess murmured, not looking up from her computer while she clicked away at the keyboard. "Enjoy the thick forests around here while you can. I'd take these one-shop towns over our stint in New York City any day. So much metal and chrome there that my tiger got cagey within minutes. At least out here I can feel the earth beneath my feet." She glanced over. "We've got a mating ceremony to officiate too, so it's not all death and doldrums."

Upon meeting Sierra and Dax, no one would assume they were mates—Sierra was a determined, serious woman while Dax had an obnoxious sense of humor that made most people want to strangle him. However, they'd somehow collided together and formed a formidable team.

"A mating ceremony? That's the worst of all," Navi grumbled.

Jess rolled her eyes. "Yes, yes, we know. You hate love. Anger, anger, roar."

Navi snorted into her pillow. Not like she could hide anything from Jess—with the amount of rooms they'd shared over the years, the woman had essentially become her sister. Every time they officiated a mating ceremony, the nausea rolled through. Not because she hated love, but because she knew the couple had stumbled onto something she would never get.

Jess put on a laid-back front, but over the years Navi watched her try and fail to keep several long-distance relationships. The phone calls slowed, texting stopped and communication faded until Navi would pull out Jess' old copy of *The NeverEnding Story* and the two of them watched the movie on repeat until her friend pretended to feel better. Navi knew better than anyone that the loneliness always remained. When she jumped from city to city, she had the clothes on her back and her Tribe—nothing else.

Even though Finn Kelly might rev her motor for now, once they hopped to the next town, he'd fade out of mind, like so many others.

* * * *

Navi stood outside the hotel, peering at the sun already sizzling the asphalt. She adjusted her pack on her shoulder before checking her phone. Asshole was five minutes late. If he planned on working with her, that bullshit wouldn't be tolerated.

A familiar Dodge Challenger veered into the lot, spraying gravel when he screeched to a halt. The Red Rocks drove like maniacs. Navi lifted her chin, full intimidation mode flipped on and fueled by irritation. He emerged from his car, the grin on his face making his umber eyes gleam and her heart stutter despite her present state of annoyance.

"I'm sorry I got held up," he said, lifting his hands. "It won't happen again." Navi's brows furrowed. She'd expected excuses, which would've sparked her temper—but, truth be told, Finn must be used to dealing with strong-willed women with Sierra as an alpha. Her annoyance fizzled out as quick as it had begun and she loped toward his car.

"Let's take your girl," she said, running her hand along the sleek frame of the Challenger. She'd give her right tit to own a beauty like that, but with the mileage they put on vehicles and the fact that her last three had been set on fire or bombed, she wasn't wasting her money. "I'm assuming she handles these country roads better than most."

His gaze heated when he focused in on her. She licked her lips before swinging over to the passenger side and tapping at the window.

"Come on," she commanded. "We've wasted enough time." Besides, if the wolfish look on his face was any indication, given much longer and they'd be liable to head straight to the bedroom, or better yet, the backseat. He'd unlocked his car, so she slipped inside, breathing in the leather scent of the interior that lingered around him. He smelled like fresh-cut grass, sweat and leather, a combination that woke her body up every time he entered a room.

Finn settled into his seat, the movement shifting the wifebeater glued to his defined abs as he started the ignition. Once the air kicked on, the sound system did too, pumping some club beats she would've never expected from him. Navi blinked a few times as he surged the Challenger forward, wheeling back onto the road.

"So, you going to fill me in on what the hell these Landsliders are and why I'm supposed to be trembling in my boots?" he asked, his gaze not veering from the winding roads he soared down.

Navi sucked in a deep breath. She hated admitting this to anyone, the shame her Tribe had kept secret for so long. Betrayal drove a deep dagger, one that made her panther snap every time she thought of it.

"Mackey was one of us — part of the East Coast Tribe. We came to blows plenty of times when we disagreed over rulings, over behavior and over the way we carry ourselves. This isn't the sort of responsibility you can shirk, and this power isn't one to be abused. He disagreed and a couple years back defected." Navi's chest squeezed tight at the loss, at the memory of the morning he'd vanished with a note left behind. For all his flaws and all the times their fights grew physical, he'd also been part of her makeshift family, one of her few constants.

"So, you're telling me one of you scary motherfuckers turned Dark Side?" Finn said, tapping his fingers against his steering wheel to the beat of the music.

Navi rolled down her window to let the breeze kiss her face and the sun soak into her skin. Gorgeous day like this, she could almost forget for a second the devastation Mackey had already caused and all that would come.

"No need to rile everyone into a panic, so the information doesn't leave us. His Landsliders get most of their money through smuggling operations and drug running. I assume you're familiar with the locals, so you'll be the one doing most of the talking at this general store. Humans might not always realize who we are, but any shifters zip up tight the second we walk into a room." Navi tugged at the front of her shirt, trying to air out the sweat pooling between her breasts. Finn looked her way for a half-second, enough to make the air blooming between them even hotter.

"Have you never seen a woman before, Kelly?" she asked, unable to help herself.

"Not one as gorgeous as you." The velvet of his voice as he fired that bit of smoothness traveled straight to her core. Most guys didn't have the balls to tango with her, because the Tribe reputation preceded her in every town they visited. Not like the reputation was any bit false — she could stop most shifters in their tracks with a single command and could manipulate water with the snap of her fingers. However, despite the Tribe she rolled with, the loneliness ate her alive some days. Just once, she wanted to meet someone bold enough to brave the flames.

She picked her nails, not looking at him. "Do those lines work on the wolves back home?"

Finn snorted. "If I was trying to charm you, you'd know. I'm as subtle as a battering ram. Honest truth is I've never met anyone like you."

"That's what happens when you live in backwater towns in central PA," Navi said, refusing to look at him with the way her cheeks heated. "I've met a dozen cocky dominants who've tried to play ball and failed."

"Any you've trusted enough to work with in the field?" he asked. Even though the question seemed innocent, she'd have to be blind to not hear the heat in his voice. The man was relentless.

"Opportunity never came up," she shot back, trying to ignore his smirk. "Think you can throw some of your persistence toward finding the Landsliders?"

"If you ask nicely," he responded, a wolfish gleam in his eyes.

Two could play at that game. Her blood boiled, but whether with irritation or lust was beyond her. She lowered her lashes. "Come on now, you won't do it for me?" she asked, her voice husky as she unleashed all the pent-up desire in her gaze.

Finn near veered off the road. The tires screeched as he zeroed back in on the asphalt ahead and tightened his grip on the steering wheel.

Navi let out a snort, the pretense dropped. "Might want to put some of that focus on driving."

Finn lifted a brow. "Woman, you're pure evil."

He drummed his fingertips over the steering wheel while they zoomed along the highway. The breezes brought the scent of grass, buttercups and diesel, an intoxicating draw to enhance this sunlit day. For a moment, Navi could pretend she wasn't on some mandated mission for the Tribe. Like she could go on a casual drive with a guy who'd piqued her interest. Except, that was a whole crock of fanciful bullshit, because her chain always squeezed tight.

Her panther stirred within her, his presence making her want to mark, to claim. She'd never felt this frenzied reaction before to any of the men she'd slept with and it wasn't just because Finn Kelly was a handsome bastard. In the distance, the three or four store stretch that made up this Podunk town cropped into view, yet another slice of Pennsyltucky.

"You're going to head in front and ask questions, use some of your charm on the owner, while I snoop around back," Navi said, clinging to the comfort of command. After endless operations like this one, she doled out orders with zero effort.

"What if the owner's a guy?" Finn teased. "Are you saying you want me to flirt with him too?"

"Guy, girl, stick — I don't care who you flirt with," she responded. "Just get a pulse on who's running the operation through their storefront."

"I feel so used." Finn smirked as he pulled in front of the general store, titled just that. Even though he caused her heart to race and her body responded to him in a way that made her heart want to follow suit, their night together hadn't meant anything.

If only telling herself that didn't feel so hollow. The sooner they resolved this Landslider problem and she was on the road and out of this town, the better.

Chapter Three

Finn strode to the front of the store, trying to think of anything but the woman slinking around back. The scent of her, the sultry look in her eyes — it made his hormones go nuclear.

He entered the old general store, the door creaking, and was greeted by the stale stench of cigars, aluminium, and what had to be days-old corn muffins. Finn had swung by here once or twice on occasion, but he didn't have much reason to go a couple towns over much less to a human-owned establishment. Shifters and humans might meld together in the cities, but out here in the country was different. Red Rocks mainly stuck to their territory lines, since humans veered away from shifters and shifters clustered around their own packs.

He slipped his hands into his pockets while he strode across the linoleum. The alliance between the Silver Springs and the Red Rocks would merge the territory of the two packs, a shift he wasn't looking forward to. Finn had agreed to follow Sierra, but, as her beta, he didn't feel full confidence in his place once she'd started going to Dax for advice and not him. His restlessness had been amped to eleven and this added fuel to the fire.

"Can I help you, son?" An older woman sat behind the counter with a Grisham novel propped open in front of her. Her leathery skin suggested hard labor outside and her dark eyes were sharp when she glanced to him. Sunlight filtered through the open windows and a large steel fan echoed with a *whup-whup-whup* throughout the store.

"Nah, I've got this," he said, flashing her a smile. "Thanks for the offer, though."

She nodded without a grin in return as she settled into her seat. He wasn't going to jump into interrogation mode without examining the storefront itself. Finn strolled through the aisles, scanning the shelves for anything out of place, a bag of charcoal briquettes in the wrong section, or cans with enough of a mark on them that no one else would bother buying them. His folks used to make drops and, if this was a site, he knew the tricks. He inhaled as he walked through. Past the normal scents he'd gathered upon walking in, he caught a hint of other shifters, faint enough he couldn't quite distinguish their animals.

That wasn't incriminating in and of itself—folks could be going in and out of this store like himself and leaving their scent. However, the odds were less likely in a human-owned store out in the middle of nowhere. Finn focused, letting the wolf ride him at the edge of turning, his fangs dropping down even though he kept them out of sight. He sank into a crouch while his hand remained on the shelving as if he were searching for something. Closer to the ground, he sniffed, trying to track any patterns.

His nostrils tingled at the scent, his wolf snapping out in aggression at the invading smells. Finn tamped the urge to growl while he followed the scent trail down the aisle, keeping out of view from the owner. He neared the section with cans of cat food, dog food, litter—all the pet basics. Right around here, the smell grew stronger, since these shifters apparently lacked ingenuity. He flipped through the boxes of dog food, noticing a couple with the tabs on the side open. Bingo.

His parents had done drops and pick-ups over the years when Ace, their meth dealer, required those runs. He recognized this protocol in action, all the tricks to avoid detection. The whole thing disgusted him all the more now that he knew what they'd been up to. Back then, he had been too young to realize the full consequence of what his parents and the other scumbags were involved with.

Time to see if the store owner's clued in on this or not.

Finn sauntered to the counter, the box of kibble in hand. He plunked it on the surface, drawing the woman's eyes from her Grisham novel yet again. A broad smile plastered his face as if he was friendly as get-all. "Just going to buy this today, ma'am."

The older woman placed the hardback on the counter and poised her fingertips over the keys of the register like she was preparing to ring him up. Her gaze settled on the mark and rip in the side of the box.

"Looks like that one's defective," she said, a touch of insistence in her voice. "Why don't you put it back and get a different one?"

Finn shrugged. "My dog will tear into the box anyway. I don't mind." He didn't budge.

A frown spread on the woman's face and those scraggly brows furrowed. "I'll get you a new one." This time, she left no room for debate in her tone, a hard edge instead. If he'd been suspicious before, he was resolute now. The owner knew what business went on in her store.

"I've got it," he said, jogging over to the display. He snagged one of the clean boxes but grabbed a can of cat food with a hefty dent and slipped the thing into his pocket. Normally, he was against shoplifting, but if this gave him a chance to get a leg up, he wouldn't waste it. Finn strode around the shelves with the regular box of puppy chow in hand for his nonexistent dog, and he plunked the kibble onto the counter before fishing out some bills.

The woman rang him up, those sharp eyes remaining on him the entire time. Her dour frown never budged from her face. Not like her lack of pleasantness mattered, because he'd gotten what he came for. Navi had wanted to confirm the drop site? Well now he had the evidence in his pocket. Finn strolled out of the general store and swung by his car to toss the box of dog food and his stolen can inside.

From where he stood, he couldn't spot Navi on either side, but then again she'd said she would be sneaking around the back. He cast a glance to the windows as he walked the length of the general store, giving enough berth to stay out of view while heading to the back. The looming trees cast their shade everywhere and a couple of beams of sunlight peeked through the leaves to imprint on the beaten earth where a car was parked, presumably the owner's.

Beyond the small lot, the woods sprawled out in every direction, the trees a rampant infestation around these parts.

He scanned the area, his wolf straining against his chest to race free through the forest. No sign of Navi. Anywhere.

Worry crawled up his arms when he crossed the clearing, scanning the ground for any sign of her. She'd said she'd be scouting around here, not vanishing completely out of sight. Besides, with his car still parked in place, she couldn't have gotten far. His heartbeat picked up a couple of notches the farther he strode along the beaten dirt patch, closer and closer to the woods. He sniffed the air around him, trying to latch on to her scent.

At the edge of the woods, dark droplets against the flat ground snared his attention. Dark, dark red on a tan canvas.

Finn crouched at once, capturing the tinny stench — he could distinguish who that belonged to in a heartbeat after the way her scent had imprinted on his mind. *Navi*.

His stomach bottomed as he stared toward the thick cluster of trees and bushes obscuring the trail ahead of him. He'd stand a much better chance of tracking her in his four-legged form.

He cast a glance behind him, but no other cars had pulled into the lot and the general store obscured the view from the road. Finn shucked his clothes off, faced the forest and let the wolf take over.

The shift rocked through him, like returning to his true skin as his body began to morph. Fur sprouted along his arms, his sight shifted to his sharper wolf eyes and he lowered to the ground on all fours. The green leaves grew more vibrant around him, the rich scents of earth, twigs and fallen leaves tickling his nose in this form. He settled onto his pads with ease. No matter how much he honed his muscles, how often he trained, he never moved with this effortless grace in his human body. Finn never felt as connected as he did when the trill of the birds filtered into his hearing, the sun heated his fur and the crickets chirped through the bushes.

He dipped his muzzle to the ground, inhaling and imprinting her scent. From this vantage point, the trail grew illuminated where it had been obscured before. The broken twigs close to the ground, the bend in the leaves ahead. The earth crumbled beneath his paws when he padded forward, following her scent. He quickened his pace farther into the woods as her trail grew clearer and clearer with every step forward. In this form, he needed to race along the land, to indulge in the urgency that had ridden his bones when he had stepped to the back lot behind the store and she wasn't there.

All the while, he remained aware of his peripheral. Whatever caused her to vanish promised danger and, with the Landsliders utilizing this place as their drop site, any one of them could sneak up on him at a moment's notice.

His surroundings whirred around him while he raced forward, the crunch of twigs, the rustle of crisp leaves, and the soft breezes rifling through his fur. He listened for any indicator of Navi even as his heart raced faster and faster, a tug-of-war between sharpened worry and the exultant joy of the run.

Up ahead, he caught the flash of dark fur.

Finn skidded to slow his pace, creeping toward the figure crouched behind the bushes.

A massive black panther prowled out from the spot, her silver eyes flashing. Finn's wolf stilled when he caught hint of the scent—Navi. Relief crashed over him. He'd never seen her shifted form, but he shouldn't have expected anything less magnificent than the panther who prowled before him now. Her sleek coat reminded him so much of the dark shade of her hair, the muscles the same coiled power, but her stature loomed even larger in this form than the compact woman he'd begun to know.

She padded over to him and nudged her forehead against his. His wolf quieted in the presence of one of the Tribe. All the power that emanated around her on a normal basis grew unleashed in this form. This was the totem animal she'd been tethered to from birth, one of the original shifter spirits the shamans had bound to humans when their kind had been created.

Finn nudged back. Even though she might be bigger and badder than he was, Finn was still a proud wolf — he didn't stand down to anyone, Tribe or no.

She tilted her head toward the general store, the direction he'd come from. Without waiting for a response from him, she took off, crossing the clearing with a couple of strides in her powerful form. Finn sprang after her, launching off his back limbs to hurtle forward. Tribe members could freeze an entire arena of shifters with their compulsion, and, hell, he'd seen folks get twitchy in their presence alone. However, Finn Kelly wasn't one to run from danger.

He raced after it through the woodlands on four legs.

Even though Navi could run with the speed and agility of a panther, Finn was no slouch, and he knew these woods with a familiarity she could never hope for.

With every faster lope forward from her, Finn gained the edge by avoiding a bush or finding the shorter route rather than looping around. Before long, he ran neck and neck with the panther, close enough to get caught up in the breeze of her steady stride, an almost mechanized smoothness to her movements. His heart pulsed with his pace, but he refused to drift behind her and let her take lead.

All too fast, the beaten dirt lot behind the general store careened into view.

Finn came to a quick halt at the same time as Navi and they turned to face one another. Her luminous eyes regarded him with a measure of respect and he puffed forward, the competitive nature of his wolf sated by having held his own.

Voices came from the front of the store — no way he and Navi could reach the car and change there. Finn slunk to the bushes and began the shift. All too fast, he returned to his human form, the fur molding to smooth skin and his bones transitioning into place, despite the tug in his chest to remain as a wolf.

His clothes lay in the crumpled pile he'd left them in and he dipped down to slide his gym shorts on before stepping out past the bushes. Navi had shifted back and, instead of the massive panther from a few moments before, she stood by the nearest oak tree in her human form, buck naked. The sun warmed the deep golden undertones of her skin and those lethal curves were on full display. Her heavy breasts and hips he wanted to grip all over again had imprinted on his memory after his one night with this woman.

"What happened to your clothes?" He smirked, walking closer to her. The droplets of her blood stained the packed earth, reminding him of the near heart attack she'd given him.

She shot him a glare. "Wasn't thinking about spares when I caught one of the Landsliders snooping around back here."

"And you didn't think of coming in to grab me?" he asked, his voice sharpening. All he'd seen was the blood and he had assumed the worst. He held his shirt in his hands, warring between his annoyance with her and the fact that she stood clutching her tits and glancing at the general store ahead. He let out a sigh and tossed his wifebeater to her.

She tugged it over her head, ruining the spectacular view. His shirt came down to her thighs and he couldn't help the surge of satisfaction at his scent marked all over her. "You had your task," she said, fixing those hazel eyes on him. "And I had mine. I'm not going to waste the time checking in when the opportunity came up. I saw the chance and took it."

"You're a gem to work with, aren't you," he responded, a slight snarl to his words. He couldn't help himself. The irritation burned through him something fierce that he'd even worried for a heartbeat when she deemed giving him any sort of heads-up too much of a bother. "It's about letting your partner know so they don't come to the back, spot your damned blood and wonder what the hell happened."

"If you're too emotional to think with a level head, I'll pick someone else to join me out here, Kelly," Navi spat with a hint of a growl edging her voice. Her hazel eyes flashed silver.

"Bull-fucking-shit," Finn argued, his fangs elongating when he faced her, arms crossed over his bare chest. "I find it hard to believe the Tribe operates like a bunch of lone wolves — that's a surefire way to end up dead." No way did she get to turn this shit around on him when she'd taken off without so much as a how-ya-do. No one in the Red Rock pack operated on their lonesome because the job wasn't worth more than a person's life, a lesson each cub learned early and one Finn had taken to heart after watching his folks waste away.

"Each of us in the Tribe has enough power that we don't need to worry about pack mentality," she threw back, the retort driving into him like a dagger. Guaranteed strategy to cut him off at the knees —

remind him how much stronger she was. How they weren't even in the same class.

"Well, then, guess you won't be needing my help," he growled. "Let's get the hell out of here."

Chapter Four

Awkward didn't come close to describing the grade-A level tension that descended in Finn's Challenger. Navi hunched forward in the seat, ready to spring out the moment they came to a halt. Her words had been harsh — she knew that. But goddamn, the concern in his eyes, how he got all worried prickled under her skin something fierce and, before she could help herself, the acid had spewed from her lips.

Finn gripped his steering wheel with enough strength to nearly rip the thing off. Even though he wasn't sniping back anymore, his anger was still palpable in the car and the way those dark eyes burned suggested he remained on the edge.

Navi sucked in a deep breath, regaining some clarity despite the guilt and irritation boiling through her. "How did your end of things turn out?" she chanced, not expecting much in the way of a response from him, since the tension stretched like a live wire between them.

"They're running something via the usual pickup routes in a nowhere town," he responded, not bothering to look at her. She lifted her brows in surprise. After his emotional outburst before, she'd expected more of the same, not this calm and collected side. "The owner made a stink when I went to buy one of them, so I bought a regular box of dog food and in the process slipped one of the marked cans into my pocket."

"Adding theft to the repertoire?" she teased, anxious to return to normal and avoid the whole ugly scene from before. Truth be told, she wasn't comfortable in the slightest at what feelings emerged the moment those brown eyes glowed with a care she wasn't used to.

His brow arched, but he didn't bother looking her way. "You're not doing that. Not with me."

"What?" she shot back, crossing her arms over her chest.

"You don't get to skate on past our fight like it didn't exist, and we're not going to play pretend," he said, his voice cool and lethal. "Either you want to work together — and work as a team — or you can cut me loose now for not fitting your definition of obedient servant."

Whatever could be said about Finn, the man wasn't lacking in guts. Few individuals possessed the bravery to mouth back to her like he did. Her abilities scared them off first and her harsh mouth second. She needed to work with someone who could view her as an equal, not a yes-man or someone too cowered to voice an opinion. As much as he pissed her off, she wouldn't find another one like him in these parts.

"Look," she said, gritting her teeth to force past the uncomfortableness prickling through her. "The Tribe doesn't hold hands and Kumbaya. Most times, when we investigate we're on our own and we accept the brunt of whatever danger is flung our way. That being said, I asked you to help, which entails working with you."

"Shocking, I know," Finn interjected, his sarcasm as hot as his temper.

Navi jutted her jaw forward. "If you're going to be a brat, I'm going to stop right here."

"Kind of tough to do when I'm driving," he retorted. She bit back her words, simmering with annoyance. When he glanced to her, his expression softened as did his grip on the steering wheel while they soared down the highway. "Fine, let's talk. What are your thoughts?"

Her brow wrinkled as she ran a hand through her relaxed strands of hair. Hell, she couldn't make heads nor tails of him. One second she was sure his temper would send her racing the opposite direction and the next the storm had departed and he was speaking sense.

"We're going to have to head to the site at night when the Landsliders aren't spooked from my pursuit, so before then, I'd say we'd better hash out some ground rules. I'm not unreasonable. If you're bringing up points to assist our mission, I'll gladly listen. Why don't we grab drinks at Beaver Tavern and figure things out over a pint?" she asked. "I'm pretty sure we could both use a brew."

Finn stiffened for a moment, but for the life of her she couldn't gauge why. Nothing she'd mentioned warranted the response.

He tapped his fingers against the side of the wheel before heaving out a sigh. "Sierra keeps spares at

Beaver Tavern, so we can change there. I could use a drink or two myself."

Navi glanced at her bare thighs, noticing for the first time that she wore his shirt, which allowed his fantastic pecs to remain on full display. With the anger cleared from her headspace, the lust returned in full force, the close proximity fueling her fire. "Don't suppose you've got a back entrance for those spares? It'd be a discredit to my surly Tribe image if I'm walking through the place in your shirt."

A different scent tingled her nose, the strong note of his arousal that made her want to moan on the spot. She didn't need to glance over to those gym shorts to notice the erection he was packing. Her panther wasn't resisting the wolfish scent of him either and, instead, the bitch preened inside her chest. Not helping her ignore the tangled web of need she'd rather leave for a rainy day. *Or never.*

"Feisty thing like you? No one would dare make a comment. Even if my shirt might as well be a dress on you," he teased, his dark eyes sparking with amusement.

Navi cracked her knuckles. "You're playing with fire, babe."

"Maybe I like the flames," he shot back while he maneuvered the Challenger right into the parking lot of Beaver Tavern.

Midday, the normal cozy glow wasn't evident, but the sun enhanced the dark wood accents of the bar and made the cream exterior even brighter. Although the place was still under construction with sections of the wall riddled with bullet holes, the Red Rocks and Silver Springs had rallied fast after Drew Williams and the Landsliders had wrecked this place. Navi had worked with packs her entire life and yet that level of togetherness baffled her. Not like she didn't work in unison with her Tribe unit once in a while, but all of them tended to operate independently.

Finn buzzed with tension again despite the resolution they'd come to and, for the life of her, Navi couldn't figure out why. He wheeled his car to park around back in the employee lot, tires crunching the gravel before he braked into Park. Navi hopped out, her bare feet tough enough for the uneven stones to not bother her much.

"Lead the way, pup," she called over to him as they crossed the lot to the back entrance where the door was held open by an orange bucket.

Finn lifted a brow at her comment, the motion tugging at the raised scar that ran right through it. He loped up the steps, his muscles moving with a piston-like efficiency. Navi followed him inside and he strode straight to a cabinet and flipped the doors open before tugging out a pair of black gym shorts and a faded gray shirt in a smaller size. He tossed them her way.

She caught them quick and slipped the shorts on first, a surprisingly decent fit, then stripped off his shirt to toss it to him. Not like his gaze left her for a second. The way his eyes burned with heat as she slipped into the new shirt scorched through her and he stood there clutching his tee without making a motion to put it on.

"Got a little drool on your lip," she drawled while she made her way through the kitchen toward the front of house. "Might want to get that before we grab a pint."

He caught up within seconds, wrestling into his shirt while they walked. "Can't help it, sweetheart. You're stunning." He said those statements like utter fact, making her flush despite herself. She'd been on the receiving end of lines that dripped with sleaze, but the sheer honesty and straightforwardness Finn spoke with was the furthest thing from contrived.

A willowy woman stepped into the doorway leading to the other side of the tavern. She had delicate Japanese features and rich black hair pulled into a bun. Her hands balled into fists at her side and she glared at Finn. He glanced up and the smile vanished from his face.

"Hey, Raven," he said, attempting casual even though his voice came out clipped.

"It's been a while, Finn," she said, her eyes darkening as her gaze settled onto Navi. "Why show up now?"

"We came for a pint," he said, ducking his head before slipping past her as if to avoid scrutiny. Navi's brows drew together on instinct and her stomach flip-flopped. Not like she had any reason to pry into his private life, but the tension between them seemed too personal — beyond a disagreement between packmates. This sheepish behavior from Finn didn't reflect the ballsy guy she'd come to respect.

The small part of her that had begun warming to him iced over. She was Tribe, temporary, and this tension between Raven and Finn was none of her concern. Even still, she swallowed hard, trying to dispel the waves of disappointment coasting over her.

"Hey," Navi said, extending a hand in greeting. "You're the bartender here, right? Can we get two pints of your darkest beer? I've got some business to discuss with this guy."

Raven glanced to the hand, and to her tattoos like shifters always did, before she gripped it and shook. "Sure thing. Take a seat, and I'll bring them right over to you." The woman plastered on a fake customerservice smile, even though the sharpness in her delicate eyes betrayed the real emotions she pinned back.

Navi wanted to be out of this bar—hell, out of this town—but she couldn't leave until they resolved the problem with the Landsliders. She felt stupid for even wasting a second of thought on Finn Kelly, when she was a passing ghost, soon to be a memory. She nodded to Raven before stepping past her and walking through the doorway to the front of house. A few glances flickered her way from the shifters at the bar and the other guys clustered around one of the tables, but they averted their eyes the moment they caught sight of the tribal markings swirling up her arms and down her legs. The normal greeting one of her kind received.

She didn't glance behind her to see if Finn followed, but headed straight for one of the round tables by the door, a smaller one tucked near the corner. Navi snagged the heavy oak chair and slipped into it. A moment later, Finn sat in the one opposite, the chair creaking when he settled down.

He cast a quick glance to the bar. "I'm sorry about that," he said, a slight flush of embarrassment staining his cheeks. "Raven and I aren't anything serious, but we've fooled around more than a couple times and I owe her a talk."

Navi clenched her jaw and her insides froze over, but she didn't betray an ounce of emotion. "That's your business, Kelly. Unless it has to do with finding the Landsliders and your ability to help me there, I don't give a damn what you're up to." Her voice came out as cool as morning frost.

Finn pressed his lips together tight as he gave a firm nod, even though those too-expressive umber eyes flashed with something like hurt. "Right. My mistake, boss."

The easy banter between them vanished in the wake of this brittleness, the tension in the air palpable. Navi's stomach twisted into knots, but she'd perfected her mask by this point. "We've got a stakeout tonight, so let's lay out some ground rules for working together."

Focusing on the job centered her. She didn't have any stake in Finn—never could—so she needed to tamp down whatever this sickening swill was.

Raven hustled in their direction with two pints in her hand and the most strained smile Navi had ever witnessed. The Asian bartender's fine features exuded a natural femininity Navi couldn't hope for. Despite her short stature, she was all brawn—her survival through the dangers she faced required her body to be a lethal weapon.

Finn stiffened at Raven's approach and the guilty way he avoided her gaze sparked Navi's temper. No way in hell would she get sucked into their interpersonal drama. He might've gripped her imagination for a half-minute, but she'd been entertaining pipe dreams. She formed a tight-lipped smile of her own as she accepted the beers from Raven. Navi placed one in front of Finn and lifted the other straight to her lips. In the midst of this awkwardness, she needed the stiff drink.

"You mind if we talk later?" Raven asked Finn, her arms crossed over her chest. The woman's nails pricked into claws, revealing how on the edge she skated.

Finn had spoken about his relationship with her like it meant nothing, so either he was the biggest idiot on the planet, or he was living in a state of perpetual delusion. Based on the guilt gleaming in those dark eyes when he looked at Raven, Navi guessed the latter.

She couldn't resist the bile rising in her throat, no matter how illogical.

"Yeah, we need to catch up to speed," he said in response, tightening his grip around the pint. He broke their eye contact to stare into the murky surface. Raven nodded, not saying another word while she slipped away as quickly as she'd arrived.

"That's barely anything to whip out the popcorn over," Navi drawled, unable to help herself.

Finn's eyes flashed. "Panther side peeking out, darling? Didn't expect that sort of cattiness from you."

"And I expected you to have a bigger set of balls," she shot back. "First impressions deceive."

She sucked in a deep breath, the acid spewing from her mouth the sort that squeezed her heart. Few managed to get under her skin like Finn Kelly, but the man had his talents. In the moment, letting her mouth run loose felt damned good, but, already, she regretted those words. What was she heckling him for? Not like she had any future with him beyond their one-night stand.

Navi took another sip of her pint to clear her head. "You're right," she said. "I'm being catty. Your relationships are none of my business. I figured the fling we had was complication-free and I'm just not comfortable getting caught in the middle of whatever you have going on with that woman. This is a temporary setting for me and we've got enough on our hands with the Landsliders."

Finn's brows rose to the point where she wondered if they'd fly clear off his face. In response to her bluntness, all his anger faded and the tension leeched from his features. He lifted a pint in her direction. "You're more than fair. I've let this mess with her go on way longer than I should've and I've been too chickenshit to confront her. However, that's my problem, not yours, and you have every reason to be annoyed."

Fuck. Every time she wanted to hate him and wanted to write him off as a forgettable lay in yet another city, he brandished honesty that disarmed her. Despite the way her veins blazed in irritation, she found communication with him easy and effortless. Not like it mattered. She'd be vacating these premises and he'd be returning to whatever confusing relationship he maintained with Raven once she left. The thought still tugged at her gut in a way she wasn't comfortable with, but in clearing the air, she'd also cleared her head.

"Let's get down to brass tacks," she said, setting her pint onto the tabletop. The near-black liquid sloshed around and the tan foam clung to the sides. "I'll be the one giving the orders. That's non-negotiable."

Finn shrugged in response. "Nothing new to me. I'm pack beta, remember?" He flattened his palms on the surface of the tabletop as those umber eyes locked with hers, sparking with challenge. "However, I'm not going to take orders from someone who can't work as a team player. I'm fine with you making the calls, but when you dash off with no heads-up while we're working a section together, I'm in the dark. And honestly, I'm a better asset informed than I am clueless to the situation and whatever dangers it entails."

Navi leaned back in her seat, arms crossed as she eyed him down. He was making fair points, ones she didn't mind putting an effort into if they could shut down the Landsliders sooner. She let out a sigh and settled forward at the table to extend her hand toward him. "It's a deal," she said.

His callused palm enveloped hers when they shook and Navi chose to ignore the spark traveling up her arm at the mere touch. The complication of him and Raven should've doused whatever flames lingered between them, but to her dismay, they still burned strong. He brought the sort of trouble and drama she avoided in every city she'd rolled through so far.

Yet despite the collision she saw coming a mile away, despite the inevitable heartbreak, hurt and wreckage he promised, Finn Kelly was a train-wreck hurtling a hundred miles an hour toward her, and she couldn't step away.

Chapter Five

Finn had made a mess of the whole situation and he only had himself to blame.

He stalked out to his car, packing the carton of cigarettes against his palm. Navi had already headed out to return to her hotel. Within seconds, he was sucking in a drag and leaning against his Challenger. Raven would be joining him out here in minutes. That meant the time had come for the confrontation he had been avoiding ever since Navi had crashed into town and he'd found himself just shy of fixated.

He loosed a stream of smoke, the flood of nicotine failing to curb the panic that threatened to descend. Sure, he should've stopped hooking up with Raven from the moment he knew there wasn't a future there. Thing was, though, they were part of a small pack, and he'd played the field during his youth. He knew what else lay out there—no one for him. And every time he thought about severing their entanglement, of being alone, that dizzying emptiness returned.

He'd never been able to shake the memories of pacing through the shoebox-sized motel rooms in the area, the ones his folks locked him in when they went on their meth runs for that lowlife Ace. Ever since those days, claustrophobia gripped him in an ugly way. The mildew scent had invaded his nostrils, the crunch of the crusted carpet beneath his feet. His wolf had raged inside his chest until he shifted, scratching at the walls with claws, hurling himself at the door until he broke out of yet another room to run free. Only to head out on the run with them again and again, rinse and repeat. He'd already been isolated from his pack — he couldn't lose his parents too.

Until he did.

Until he walked into one of the hotel rooms to find them cold and turning a pale blue on the floor, courtesy of Ace and his crew. Those were the very bastards who'd roped them into that business in the first place and the ones Finn swore he would someday tear apart with his own claws.

He let out another stream of smoke, ash tumbling off the end of his cigarette. Down that path lay memories he'd rather forget, of a time and place he'd shut away a long time ago.

Raven emerged from around the back of Beaver Tavern, her steps measured with the agility of a wolf. She didn't have the slink to her step Navi did, the fluidity that mesmerized Finn, but, like any predatory shifter, she could approach quietly. She'd undone her thick black hair from the bun she kept it coiled in behind the bar and her hands balled into fists, as if she summoned her own determination. He'd seen the hurt sparking her dark eyes in the tavern. Finn felt like shit.

That was the exact outcome he'd been looking to avoid. Like he could.

To make matters worse, Navi had iced over, the growing connection with her severed.

Finn finished his cigarette and ground it under his heel when she approached. "Why don't we talk in private?" He cast a glance to the open windows of Beaver Tavern. As much as the pack liked sticking their noses in his business, the conversation between him and Raven was none of theirs.

"Let's head to our old spot," Raven said, her eyes flashing the silver of her wolf. "I'll race you there."

His heart squeezed at the thought of the spot they'd met at through their teenage years, through fumbling makeouts to escapes when the old alpha would jaw off too much over their obligations or one of them picked a fight for the thousandth time. The pack elders had run bets on who'd survive through to adulthood between him, Raven and Jer. The three of them had broken the rules and pulled the sort of risky shit in their youth that skated the line of stupid.

"All right," he said, cracking his knuckles in front of him. He could use the run right now. He stripped off his shirt and his jeans dropped to the ground seconds later as his skin prickled with the beginnings of his change. Raven folded her black tank top and skirt from work and placed them on the ground, the gorgeous woman's nudity nothing new for him. He'd seen and tasted every square inch of her body.

Finn's claws emerged, the fur overtook his skin and his bones morphed as he shifted for the second time that day. His wolf stretched out with pleasure at the opportunity to run free. In this form, his world enhanced in every feasible way. His senses intensified the trill of the birds through the trees, the zoom of distant cars approaching down the highway and the whistle and creak of the branches from the gusts of wind.

Raven shifted into her sleek form, slightly smaller than his, with a dark, almost black coat apart from a couple of streaks of gray. She tilted her head in his direction, her eyes flashed silver and she bolted into the forest.

Finn dove in after her, the leaves compressing beneath his paws, the wind whistling through his fur and pebbles spraying out of his way. The midday sun gleamed through the thick forest, creating a dappled display of light on the woodland ground. Even with the scent of thick moss, of the earth that tingled his nose and the way nature tamed his beast, he couldn't halt the turmoil in his head.

Not like his wolf agreed. The beast in him viewed things in black and white and from the beginning when he'd first flirted around with Raven, he hadn't felt more in his chest than a fierce friendship. He loved her — he always would — but her similar nature had provided a comfort, a mutual sharing of the shit paths their lives had taken them. And they'd remained in a toxic cycle for so, so long, clinging to each other for dear life.

The intense way his wolf blinked to awareness when Navi entered a room was the sheer opposite, the take-notice chemistry that gripped him by the throat. And the sort that made it all too clear he and Raven had been wasting their time together for far longer than they should've.

He slowed the moment he caught the flash of the old wooden picnic table in their clearing. Raven switched to a trot, not serious about the race. In fact, she didn't look excited about the talk they would be having either, as if they both sensed the impending storm on their horizon. Finn sniffed the ground when he came closer, the scents of Jer, Raven and countless other pack members from his generation mingling here.

Finn came to a halt in front of the varnished trunk which sat beside the old picnic table and the hewn stumps everyone used as seats. Even though he hadn't been here in a long while, the site got use, evident by the scorched earth from their campfires and the emptied bottles of whiskey. He shifted back, almost shaking out of his fur as he stood up to two feet. The claws retracted, morphing back to nails.

"You think the clothes we stashed are still around here?" Finn asked, rummaging around in the trunk, which had gotten chewed into by squirrels. He brushed over balls of crumpled-up clothing they'd stored here, but with the damage and weathering, they were the crunchy sort of musty he wasn't keen on throwing on.

"Depends on where this conversation is heading," Raven said from behind him, her thigh brushing against his side when she crouched beside him. The plum and clear-water scent of her was so familiar, so safe, and he didn't miss the suggestive note in her voice. Because like her, a part of him prepared to submit to their usual modus operandi.

He tossed on the shirt, wrinkling his nose as the starchy fabric settled over his skin, dust and grit cascading from it. Raven snatched another old pair of spares from the trunk while he pulled on the shorts. Tension brimmed from her in spades and that storm-cloud wouldn't be retreating any time soon.

However, if he wanted to break this chain, he needed to begin now. His stomach tightened as he settled onto one side of the picnic table, leaning on the splintered surface.

"Look, I know we talk about anything but us," he started, flexing his fingers in front of them, since he suddenly found his nails fascinating. "We need to, though."

Raven took a seat on the opposite side of the picnic bench, her quietness unsettling. Not like he expected her to be chatty — the woman hated idle small talk — but this was a loaded silence. The nearby stream murmured in the background, the sound growing louder in this absence of communication between them. Finn's skin itched and he shifted in his seat. If she didn't say something soon, he would have to plow right through the silence.

"I know we never discussed being exclusive," she said, her voice hesitant. The hurt there broke him. He wanted her mad, wanted her claws out and her eyes flashing pissed — that he could work with. Raven contained more strength than these weak displays, than bending when she should be standing strong. Hell, he put on just as bad a front. He had no problem barreling into danger or going head to head with his alpha, yet this relationship broke him every time, like he was nine years old again and stepping into the room reeking of death and decay. Like if he didn't grip on to whatever lifeline he could, he'd end up in a motel room, alone.

"Your scent was all over her," Raven murmured.

"She put on one of my shirts," he argued, even though he knew what she meant. "We shifted earlier and her clothes got left behind." Except even with all the time he and Raven spent together, the hundreds of times they'd hooked up, his scent had never imprinted on her. That was reserved for true connections and he'd be an idiot to deny what bloomed between him and Navi.

"You know she can't stay," Raven warned as she clutched tight to the park bench beneath her. "She's Tribe, so once her business ends here, she'll be leaving and it's not like you can go with her."

His throat tightened. He and Navi had never discussed a future, never contemplated anything beyond a one-night stand. Because deep down, they knew that was all they could ever have. She was Tribe and he was Red Rock's beta. They had found their roles, and those were cemented into place.

Except her arrival shifted his views, opening his mind. He'd been so focused on the past that he'd clung to the relationship with Raven, which wasn't helping either of them. He opened his mouth, knowing what he needed to say and what he needed to do, but the words stuck like glue.

Raven's brows furrowed, as if she could see the inevitability on his face. "Take the time you need to with her," she said. Her lips formed a thin line afterward and the unhappiness was broadcast clear on her face, in her voice. "You know I'll always be around."

Finn's gut twisted at how she cared so little about herself. He leaned forward, tilting her chin until their eyes met. "You're worth more than this, Rae. We're using each other as safety nets at this point and it's not helping either of us."

Her lower lip trembled. "I'm not sure I could survive without this."

Fuck. With the hellish shit she'd been through when she ran away from the pack, he knew what demons she fought every day. He was one of the only people on this planet who did. The weight of that burden settled on his shoulders every time he considered walking away, every time he prepared to break off their complicated relationship. Because at the end of the day, he would never be in love with her and she would always be in love with him.

"Enjoy your time with her while you've got it," Raven said, running a hand through her thick black hair. Even in the crusted tee she wore, three sizes too big, the woman had a sloping, delicate beauty, from her oval face to her small, slender nose. "Just don't cut me out."

He clenched his jaw, hissing out a sigh. "Even if I had someone else in my life, our friendship doesn't have to die." She met his eyes with a knowing that twisted his gut. They both knew he spewed utter bullshit. With their history and the depth of Raven's feelings, an ordinary friendship would never be on the table — not for them.

"Just...take your time with her," Raven repeated, the hoarse scrape of her voice revealing the pain. No version of this situation would make her happy, unless he swore his undying commitment to her. That would never happen, and they both knew the truth. He had tried to be clear with her on how far his feelings extended, and she'd begged him to stay anyway.

The longer he stayed here, the more he'd be tempted to fall into the patterns of the past. Finn leaned forward and mussed her hair, causing her to wrinkle her nose. "Raven, I just want to see you happy," he said before tugging the crusty shirt off and tossing it into the trunk. "I've got a stakeout to attend, but I want you to think on that — what your happiness is separate from me."

He didn't look back to witness the disappointment on her face as yet again he failed her. He ditched the shorts and shifted into his wolf form before taking off into the deep forest, heading toward Beaver Tavern.

* * * *

Finn had barely returned to his car when his phone started buzzing. By the time he jumped into the driver's seat, the ringing had already stopped, adding to the other five missed calls from Navi. Several texts crowded his inbox too, so he settled into the seat and scrolled through the first one. All the text said was *Meet me at the general store. Now.*

He jammed his keys into the ignition and tore down the highway, unable to quell the nerves rushing through him. The way Navi threw herself into danger triggered every protective instinct in him, even though she was Tribe, capable and a hell of a lot stronger than him. He pressed harder on the gas pedal, sending his girl rocketing faster, farther. Navi wasn't the sort for dramatics — in fact, she leaned toward the extreme opposite — so if she contacted him, trouble was a guarantee.

The setting sun sprawled out across the horizon, those amber, rose-gold and ruby streaks painting the skyline in front of him. This day had passed by in a whirlwind of problems and he'd raced through it from beginning to end. Yet, despite the confrontation with Raven not having been the firm step he needed to make and the way the clash with Navi at the bar had twisted up his insides, Finn felt a distinct change. The restlessness, the itch under his skin that had begun to grip him on a daily basis had vanished.

Since he'd been working alongside Navi, purpose had seized him by the throat and hadn't let go. He'd been searching for that ever since he'd become beta of the Red Rocks.

All too soon, the stretch of buildings of the next town cropped into view. Finn had barely entered when he spotted the problem. When the wail of sirens filtered in through his open windows.

The general store was going up in flames.

Chapter Six

Focusing on the job had been Navi's best avenue after she'd left Finn at the bar with his girl, since the two of them obviously had a talk in store. Not like she cared. Well, that was a load of horseshit—not like she should care. However, when she'd hopped in the Plymouth and headed into town to scope out the best avenues through the woods, a much bigger distraction had smacked her in the face.

The general store was burning down.

Flames licked the surface of the store, climbing up the old wood with a vengeance. The charred scent of burning cedar tingled her nose even from the distance and oily tufts of blackened smoke rose to the sky. The heat threatened summer's own, battling the humidity with every gust like forge billows. She'd called the human authorities at once, since a human-owned store fell under their jurisdiction, despite the shifter interference. Then she'd called Finn, willing the charming bastard to pick up his phone, and left messages when he hadn't.

Time to get to work.

The burning building was beyond her control, but she could keep the flames from spreading to the nearby stores. If the fire moved, the rest of the town would go up like tinder. Navi loped around the back of what looked like an ice-cream shop and prowled back and forth in search of a bucket lying around. No dice.

Except she had other avenues. Navi climbed the back steps. The moment she rattled the knob to find the door locked, she altered her nail into a claw and began jimmying the lock. It clicked open and she shoved her way inside. Even in the darkened kitchen of the place, her panther eyes could see with ease and she slunk over to the sink where underneath lay a bucket that she filled with water to start. She'd summon the rest once she got there.

Dampen any tendrils of flames crawling closer. Reach out with my powers to pull the water from the ground. Refill the bucket. Continue the cycle.

Sweat poured down her forehead from the heat from the fire, warmth from the summer night and sheer exertion. Navi didn't falter. Until the fire trucks arrived, she needed to keep the flames from spreading. It wasn't until she heard the first wail of the sirens that she stopped in the middle of summoning more water.

Navi jogged up, droplets of sweat tickling while they trickled down her forehead, her neck, her arms. Her tank top plastered to her chest with sweat from the humidity and the heat from the fires. The firefighters set to work at once, a swarm of efficiency as the squad attached the hose and got the water flowing. By the time she made it to the roadside, the first jet of water blasted into the general store.

The red-and-blues flashed and a police car pulled up around the same time, coming to a screeching halt in front of her. A wide-eyed officer hopped out, the sort of green she'd expect out here. Navi didn't hesitate as she trekked in his direction, wiping the sweat from her forehead and sweeping the strands of her pixie cut back in place. As the governing force on the shifter side, she'd had plenty of run-ins with human law enforcement. Even though they packed silver bullets to handle her kind, in a one-on-one fight, she'd always have the edge. Tribe members didn't intimidate.

"Investigating a trafficking ring amongst my species, Officer," Navi called out, stepping in front of him before he approached the firefighters. No need to waste time. "I'm thinking the bastards I'm tracking down are behind this arson."

The officer eyeballed her, pausing on the tattoos up and down her arms. "Your kind did this?" he said, far from incredulous. "I'm going to need to verify your identity — standard protocol and all."

Her gaze heated and, based on the way his hand jumped to his pistol, her eyes must've flashed silver. With the amount of shifters living around here, the law enforcement should've been used to her kind — except from what she'd seen, the two species tended to stick to their own turfs.

"Navi Tremere of the East Coast Tribe," she said with a smile, extending her fangs for extra emphasis. The man near dove into his car before punching the information through the system, the screen illuminating his pasty skin. Even if the cops gave her a little trouble at first, once her credentials followed through, humans stepped the hell in line. For that matter, shifters did, too.

The cop slunk out of his car again, his gaze skating the ground as he refused to make eye contact with her. A member of the Tribe, Navi's powers placed her high on the food chain, but those abilities came at a price. No one wanted to be friends with a monster.

"Ms. Tremere, feel free to continue with your investigation. I will forward any information we find regarding the arson your way," he said, growing docile like the rest. In fact, only one man had the brass balls to treat her like an equal—like she was normal. Yet he remained wrapped up with his piece from the past and none of her business.

Navi swallowed, hard, and nodded. "Appreciate the help. I'll see if the culprits are within running distance."

Headlights on this lonely street drew her attention past the blare of the sirens and the rotating red, white and blues. A familiar Dodge Challenger came to a screeching halt yards away, since no one in the Red Rock pack could drive like a sane person.

Navi didn't bother saying goodbye to the cop, just walked toward Finn's car. Even though the adrenaline from trying to quell the flames had petered out when the fire truck appeared, her heart picked up speed the second the handsome bastard stepped out of his car. He wore the same tee from earlier, too well, as the honed muscles of his upper arms were on clear display with his rolled sleeves. His umber eyes near glowed with concern when he met her halfway.

"Looks like the assholes from this morning took notice of our visit." Navi hooked her thumbs through the belt loops and rocked back and forth on the balls of her feet.

Finn swiped a hand over his buzz cut, his mouth twitching. "Fuck, I saw the texts and thought something happened. The old biddy who owned the shack was a shady bitch — I'm just glad you're okay."

Navi winked. "That's cute, babe. You do realize I could knock out most folks with my pinky, right?" A prickle of a flush rose regardless, one she was grateful didn't show for an inch.

He shrugged. "Doesn't mean I can't worry."

Damn the man. And damn me for reacting when I need to be retreating. No drama and no attachments, the two rules she'd followed her entire life when it came to hook-ups. Finn Kelly somehow threatened those rules in every way possible, even though she'd trained herself in shutting people out. Navi thanked the Spirits she hadn't felt the mating bond snap into place. If she ever ended up with a mate, her ship was beyond sunk.

"Well, if you're done dragging your heels, we've got work to do," she said, tilting her head toward the woods behind the general store. He loped past her, those long legs outpacing her tread in seconds.

"Waiting on you, sweetheart," he said, flashing her a smile. The hungry gleam returned to his eyes, so different from the sheepish awkwardness she'd dealt with before — this was the predator she'd come to respect.

Navi jogged to catch up, directing them away from the path through the woods they'd traveled before. Chances were, the Landsliders would have left someone as sentry to send the heads-up of any further investigation. They might not have realized the pot they stirred in attempting to outsmart Navi Tremere, but they would soon.

Navi and Finn passed the ice-cream shop, and she directed them past another empty lot to where the woods thickened, closer to the section she'd uncovered earlier. Navi stepped to the edge of the forest, the leaves scraping around her ankles and the long grasses brushing at her calves.

"Shift," she commanded as she stripped off her shirt and shorts and tossed them to the ground. Even as Finn did the same, she could feel his gaze on her, a brand she didn't want to admit she liked.

Given the timing of the blaze, whatever idiots had set the storefront on fire couldn't have gotten far on feet or paws. She didn't give a damn if they were the fastest wolves in the region. She was a panther. She was Tribe.

Navi shifted, the switch as natural as breathing. Her tattoos kept the wild side of her close to the surface even in human form, so the change rarely affected her. That black and white nature, the aggressiveness and the enhanced senses were always close at heart. Her hands turned to paws, she sprouted vicious claws and the thick fur coated her body when she settled onto all fours.

In this form, doubts didn't cling to her, worries faded away and the hunter's clarity settled in. The whole change was addictive. Too many times she'd shifted into panther form and sometimes for so long she forgot how to be Navi Tremere.

A huff came from behind her as a big silver and rust wolf approached. *Finn.* Navi took the first couple of steps toward the woods, padding across the dry leaves and soft dirt. Already, she caught the scent of unfamiliar shifters on the breeze. She nudged her muzzle forward, catching Finn's gaze, those piercing eyes that seared right through her.

Together, they ran.

As the breeze filtered through her fur and the mud churned under her paws, the joy of the hunt swept through. In their haste, these shifters had been sloppy. Their scent marked everywhere with no effort to hide it and branches were bent, leaves trampled. Even though Finn lagged a couple of feet behind, he made a valiant effort to keep up. Her panther form was bigger and thick corded muscles burst with energy, so, at a flat run, she outpaced. The forest quaked where she landed and, in this form, the raw power of the panther spirit-bonded to her radiated through.

Navi slowed upon reaching a stretch of caves with openings that swallowed darkness. The scent trail led straight up to the entrances. Even with her enhanced vision, she couldn't make out what lingered in those black holes. She paced the ground in front of the entrance, unable to quell her suspicion. The Landsliders might be in a panic, but they hadn't been complete idiots so far. Backing themselves into a corner would snap a noose around their necks, meaning this was a trap. Diving in would be sheer lunacy.

Finn sailed past her, not pausing for a heartbeat.

Into the depths of the cavern he plunged, disappearing from sight. Her heart slammed as her muscles tensed to leap. Not like she could leave him to get eviscerated on his own inside. He'd made their choice the second he thundered in. Navi let out a low growl that reverberated through her chest before racing into the caves after him.

The air was stale and cool, the dust swirling around her feet when she bounded inside. With the light vanished, her other senses took over. The scent of the Landsliders threatened to overwhelm here and, apart from the pounding of Finn's feet ahead of her, slight rustles from the side of the cavern stole her attention. The moment he passed them, they'd launch their attack.

Damn it all.

Navi let out a loud roar, one that quaked the small cavern. The reverberations shook the loose stones, making them clatter onto the floor.

Finn skidded to a halt, and just in time. In the seconds they'd been inside, her eyes had begun adjusting to this darkness and inky shapes surged from behind a rocky crag. The spirit of the panther inside rushed to the forefront, demanding quick and terrible retribution. Despite the way her Great Spirit tried to override her over and over again, Navi maintained an iron grip.

Another cave-shaking roar exploded from her mouth as she rocketed forward. Even though Finn would get a tongue lashing when they were done, she wasn't about to let the Landsliders tear him to shreds.

She charged toward the figures on the other side of the cavern, three by her estimation, even though she could barely make out the forms in the liquid dark. Their ragged breaths came out in rasps as the Landsliders burst past their cover. A black bear thundered toward her, ready to attack, but Navi wasn't in the mood to play.

The other two shifters lunged for Finn, wolves by the sleek shape of their figures. He let out a snarl that echoed through the cavern and leapt for the nearest one. His sharp teeth descended and he latched on to the wolf's neck.

Before the black bear could rush into her, Navi pivoted around to ram headfirst into him. The shifter let out a low roar, skidding a couple of paces under the force of her blow. The bear's solid muscle didn't stand a chance against her thick skull. Three shifters had been lying in wait for them here. Her stomach twisted. Seemed off — three made for a pitiful trap.

The bear lunged for her, slashing with those sharpened claws. Navi remained fluid and ducked out of the way with ease. She slammed her paws to the ground, tapping into the Great Spirit she was bound to as the power rushed through her.

"Stop," Navi called out, unleashing a roar of a command. The bear halted mid-stride, the compulsion binding him on the spot. As Tribe, this was their most important tool in governing the packs, the damage control necessary against shifters who'd worked themselves into a frenzy. Otherwise, stepping in the middle of a riot of claws and fangs was tantamount to suicide.

Except, after a second of freezing, the bear swiped for her again.

Navi snapped to attention — too late. Those vicious points sank in past her fur before Navi could skid back. Ice filtered through her veins. Her command should have worked. Her Tribe compulsion had always — always — worked in the past. The wolves hadn't responded to her order, either, and both of them snapped their jaws at Finn, pushing him closer and closer to the opposite wall of the cavern. Whatever change allowed this, Navi knew in her bones this had everything to do with their rogue Tribe member, Mackey Kendricks.

The scent of blood from where the bear had swiped did little more than enrage her panther and, before the beast made another attempt, Navi pounced. She was claws, fangs and fury.

Under the onslaught, Finn scrambled back as fast as possible, farther and farther into the cavern. Except he only had so far to go before the shifters backed him against the wall. Navi crouched down and surged forward again. Her head slammed into the bear, sending him staggering to thud against the cavern's side. *Enough wasting time.* These shifters had been left as distraction. She whipped around to where the wolves pressed in on Finn. Navi launched forward.

Even outnumbered, the Red Rock beta put up a fierce fight. He rammed into one of the wolves, only to pivot back around right when the other descended. Even still, he'd only accumulated a couple of scratches. Navi gave no warning, with a quiet approach only her kind could accomplish. She crashed down between the two wolves right as they reared to lunge for Finn. With their backs turned, they didn't see her in time.

Swipe. Smash.

One swayed from the force of her blow, but, before the other could respond, Navi rerouted, smashing the beast in the side. The wolf lost his footing, skidding across the uneven ground to land with a crash. Finn didn't pause. His gaze flashed when he caught sight of her, and he followed through her initial attack by leaping upon the wolf. The bear crept behind her — she could hear those plodding footsteps — but he was sorely mistaken if he thought he could sneak up unnoticed.

She rebounded off the nearest boulder surface to whip around and face the bear shifter fool enough to take her on. Gravel sprayed in the wake of her fast motions.

The moment she turned, a slight beep pricked her hearing, one that pierced through the whole cavern.

A second later, a boom came from the front of the cavern and the ground shook under her feet.

Chapter Seven

The second those rocks began to fall, Finn's heart threatened to burst out of his chest. He lunged forward, away from the wolves and away from even Navi as he bolted toward the entrance. He needed to get out of there. Couldn't escape.

Once he'd seen the trail leading to a cave, he'd dived straight in, because otherwise he wouldn't have gone. Fear would have paralyzed him, like it had the countless times his parents had trapped him in those motel rooms. Ice crawled through his veins, ruffling his fur. In the wake of the explosion at the mouth of the cave, both wolves he'd been tangling with abandoned the fight. Both of them darted in that direction. Navi bypassed the other shifters, racing toward the tumble of stones and rock, as if somehow the massive panther could stop them from falling.

Finn paced back and forth, trying to stave the fear choking him and his wolf alike. *No escape.* The rocks had barred the entrance, sending billowing gusts of dust and grit to roil around the space. Instead of running to help the shifters knock away stones and fallen debris, he backed away until he hit the cave wall. The coldness of the stone leeched into his spine. All too fast, the space grew much smaller, the air thicker. He thrashed, both he and his wolf unable to quell the buzzing in his mind that turned into a roar.

The Landsliders might've been desperate to tear them to shreds mere moments before, but all three had abandoned the pursuit the moment the stones had started tumbling. They focused on kicking rocks out of the entryway, trying to find a gap in the barrier. By the frenzied way they clawed, they hadn't expected to get buried in this cave. He stamped his paws and dug into the ground in front of him.

Had to escape.

Had to find a way out.

Except each time he tried to place a paw forward, his vision swirled. *Fuck.* He was so fucking weak. So fucking useless. Every effort to lunge snapped back on him, until he crouched against the wall, paralyzed.

Navi's massive paws sent stones flying and she slammed her body into the larger rocks, the panther moving any bit of rubble she could away from the entrance. The woman turned into a relentless battering ram when she dove toward the barrier over and over to hammer away at the stones and grit barring their escape.

What a pointless effort. They'd die here. They'd lose what oxygen remained and end up bloated bodies on the cavern floor. He'd be trapped here for good. The hysteria bubbled inside him and low growls emitted from his throat unbidden.

Navi's deep silver eyes fixed on him for a moment. Even as the other three shifters continued hurling themselves into the wall of loose stones and rubble, she padded away from it. In his direction.

Finn tried to surge forward as frustration burned him from the inside out. Fear restrained him like a collar around his throat.

Navi approached, her steps silent as the crunch and creak of tumbling stones sounded in the background while the other shifters fought against the landslide. She nudged him with her forehead, the gentle contact jarring. Finn tried to suck in deep breaths though he panted on reflex. She nudged at him again, the heat and power radiating from her as she nuzzled him in a tender way he'd never expected from the sharp, lethal woman.

The feel of her fur against his and the sheer weight of her presence provided a balm to his nerves. Even though every glance to the closed-off entrance ahead sent a jolt of terror through his veins, he managed one step forward. Then another. His wolf responded to her with a gut-wrenching pull he'd never received from another soul. Her status as Tribe didn't have anything to do with it—Navi reached him in a way no one else ever had.

Finn took another couple of steps toward the cave-in, keeping his gaze down while he tried to focus on his paws, each movement forward. Navi remained by his side, her sleek form rubbing against him as she urged him ahead. He kept his snout down, sniffing the ground as he went, trying to catch a wisp of fresh air despite the staleness and dirt threatening to overwhelm. Even though Navi could be putting a massive dent at the cave-in, far more than the

Landsliders managed, she stayed back with him. Navi kept in contact the entire time, slowing her approach to match his tentative steps. Her presence, her touch offered the one thread of sanity he clung to while his wolf howled and the animal side of him fought to frenzy.

He followed the length of the cave-in to the far left, away from where the other shifters threw themselves into digging. Here, his nose pricked with the tickle of fresh air. If he could cling to that, maybe he could push past this useless fear and his fucking freeze-up. Some beta he made. No wonder he wasn't alpha of the Red Rocks.

Focusing on the thread of air, Finn dug.

Rocks flew underneath his paws as he channeled the anxiety, the dread and the choking shame into the motions as they turned frenetic. Navi joined him, but instead of throwing rocks like before, she slammed her paws to the ground. At first, nothing happened. The sight of her intense concentration distracted him from the skittering sensation threatening to tug him under.

A moment later, tendrils of water emerged from the cracks in the ground, pooling beneath her paws. If his tunneling hadn't become automatic at this point, he would've stopped in mid-dig. *Not like I should've been surprised.* She was Tribe — it was a matter of time before she used the elemental magic the shamans had bestowed on her. The water gathered into a pool around her paws and she pushed the liquid forward. Rivulets trickled around the stones in front of them, the water finding a way through the cracks their claws couldn't latch on to.

Finn caught on to what she was attempting. Where she loosened the stones, he focused his dig, sending more pebbles sailing behind him, even though his paws chafed and his claws had been pared down. He let out a howl, drawing the attention of the other shifters. They wasted time slugging away at the thicker part of the rockslide when their efforts could be put to better use. With how slick the water grew around him, he stumbled several times and mud stained his fur while he continued to slog away at the pile of rocks.

Navi gave them a way out.

The trickle of water slipped through the stones, finding the path of easiest resistance, which meant the more he focused on that section of rubble, the faster they could get to fresh air. The faster they could escape this prison.

Ragged breaths escaped his throat in pants as he launched into the task of digging himself out, his vision tunneling straight ahead to the stones in front of him. He breathed in the grit, the stale air and the edge of nickel and copper woven through the stone. Under the strain of the flowing water, smaller stones tumbled away, clearing the path. Navi crouched in front of the pile, her eyes closed in concentration and her paws pushed forward as she coerced the flowing water. If he hadn't seen those powers with his own eyes, he'd barely have believed in them.

The water flowed with more urgency as more of the stones spilled out of the way, the smaller ones tumbling past him to the ground. Finn's skin beneath his fur prickled and he drank in the fresh air. As it circulated through his lungs, the sharp gasp of outside took the edge off his panic. A creak sounded as larger pieces of granite and shale rolled past him, a few clipping him in the side. The water burst through and the rockslide shifted.

Finn didn't duck. Instead, he wedged himself into the spot before more stone could crush into place. Rocks pelted his back, but he shrugged off the pain, digging with a fury. The first crack of moonlight spilled in from the cave-in, tremulous and silvery. The water stilled when Navi took a step back, no longer shoving it forward with her powers. A moment later, she joined him in slamming her body at some of the bigger rocks barring their way. The other three shifters set to work beside them, a circle of grunts and whines sounding through the air, followed by the *thunk* as more debris hit the sides of the cave.

As several of the larger rocks crashed out of the way, the gap leading to the outside widened. Finn dipped his muzzle through, kicking off with his back paws to push himself out. More rubble cascaded from the opening while he thrashed through the pile-up, ignoring the scrape of stone. The urge to escape drove him with such a ferocity he didn't care. The moment his front paws hit the earth outside the cave, he dug his claws in and kicked again to vault through.

Once he stood under open sky studded by thousands of silver stars, Finn's heart quieted, and his adrenaline cooled. His ribcage shuddered as he drew in steadying breaths. Out here, he could be bold, he could be brave — a whole horizon of possibilities.

A minute later, Navi leapt through the hole, pebbles spraying in the wake of the force. She landed to the ground with the brunt of her weight, causing clouds of dust to roil around her.

The wolves squeezed out one after the other and the black bear pushed through even as more stones clattered out behind him.

Except Finn already stepped in front of the shifters in a crouch, muscles tensed for a fight. He let out a low warning growl.

The wolf closest to him mutated, fur rippling and the form changing when he shifted into his human form. The other one hunched down to do the same, transforming back onto two feet. If they bothered to shift to their weaker sides, that meant they wanted to talk.

Finn settled to begin the shift despite the complaint from his wolf who wanted to remain in this form a little longer. If he always indulged his wolf, he'd rarely be on two feet. Over the years, Finn's wild side had commanded more and more attention, and with the way the restlessness had ridden him lately, he shifted to clear his head. His limbs elongated and, as he returned to his human form and the adrenaline faded, the abuse he'd put his body through began to make an appearance. Bruises coated his arms, his nails were bloody and chipped and his hands chafed raw.

Navi took the cue and shifted too, from the sleek form of her panther to the curvaceous woman he couldn't keep his eyes off. He hadn't forgotten what she'd done for him in the cave, not for a moment.

"Don't even think of moving," he called out, flexing his arms in front while he settled back in his human body. After freezing inside the cave, he was finished with feeling like a sack of shit. *Time for action.* "I can guarantee I'm faster and I won't hesitate to shove you inside the tomb and seal up the exit."

"We were supposed to be the distraction while they circled around and launched an attack after you entered," the brunette chick who'd been a wolf spoke up. Her thick brows furrowed, causing lines of strain on her otherwise smooth face. "No one made mention that we were disposable."

A shorter, stout guy with a bulky frame spat on the ground as he approached, his ruddy skin flushed and a nasty bruise marring his stomach. "If they're willing to sacrifice our lives, we don't owe them allegiance." Even as those two spoke, the other wolf shifter remained silent, his features pensive. Finn didn't trust him for a second.

"Are you taking orders from Mackey directly?" Navi asked, stepping up beside Finn. She crossed her arms over her chest and fixed the shifters with the weight of her intimidating Tribe stare.

The brunette shook her head, her shoulders slumping in defeat. "He's too high up on the food chain to get involved with this sector." She opened her mouth again, glancing quickly at the other wolf shifter, the guy who could have bored holes into walls with the intense glare he gave her.

"Don't look to him for answers," Finn interjected, drawing her attention front and center. "He's not going to determine whether you walk out of this clearing alive. Even if you didn't rat out the Landsliders, do you think they'd keep you?"

The stout guy stepped past her, ignoring both of his companions. "Dale Rossi's the one in charge of the operations around here. I hope you find him and drive a stake through his heart. He's been holding my auto shop hostage, but that's not worth a damn if I'm dead. You're welcome to raid Jared's Auto up the road once I gather my stuff and get the hell out of here." He shook his head, his brows drawn with the grim look on his face.

Finn jerked to attention at the name. He couldn't place where he'd heard of the guy before, but the mere mention sent a chill down his spine.

The motion happened so fast they didn't see it coming.

The surly wolf mutated his nails into claws and lunged for the bear's throat.

As the bear shifter turned to face his betrayer, the claws sliced deeper, right across the jugular. Blood sprayed.

Finn didn't hesitate. His growl split the air when he lunged. Before the guy could extract his claws and before he could take a step in the opposite direction, Finn slammed a fist to his sternum. He pivoted around to wing an arm around the man's throat, the motion fluid with his dance. His muscles squeezed tight as he wrapped his arm around the man's windpipe. Wheezes followed and Navi stepped right in front of them.

Footsteps pounded from behind as the brunette rushed through the bushes to escape, but she wasn't top priority right then. The bear shifter collapsed to the ground, clawing at his neck while blood gushed from his throat. Once Finn saw where those claws had sliced, he knew the man would die.

"Since you've taken away the one solid lead we had," Navi said, crossing her arms, "you'll have to start talking."

"Try and command me," he rasped, daring her. Finn squeezed tighter around the man's throat, not giving him an inch.

Navi's eyes narrowed, clearly annoyed. "Then you'll die," she said, her tone frosted over.

Finn quirked a brow, surprised at the change of heart. If the man went back to the Landsliders, he doubted they'd welcome him with open arms. This jackass was as dead as the guy he'd murdered anyway. He clenched his jaw, summoning the nerve while he placed the heel of his hand against the man's chin with his other arm still wrapped around the guy's neck.

"Any last words?" she asked, the cold justice in her voice what he associated with Tribe.

The man clung to his stubbornness, not responding. Navi lifted her hand, claws forming in place of her fingertips. Only fitting. Except, she probably had to deliver more executions in her life than anyone should be burdened with—and who knew what age that responsibility had started. The man was one snap away from a quick death in Finn's hands. He would take whatever weight he could off that remarkable woman's shoulders.

Gritting his teeth, he slammed the heel of his hand against the man's jaw. His head snapped and, in the same moment, Finn squeezed tight around the neck with his other arm. The crack resounded through the clearing, the snap reverberating through him.

The man slumped in his arms as the life blinked out of his eyes. Finn let him drop to the ground with a thud. He wished he could feel more remorse over what he'd done, but he had no reservations about the kill or be killed part of survival—one thing he and his wolf were in wholehearted agreement on.

"You didn't have to do that," Navi said, her voice quieting. Their eyes met for a moment, the understanding a charged current between them.

"And you didn't have to help back there," he murmured, his voice hoarse with seriousness. Navi pressed her full lips together and she tucked a stray piece of her pixie cut behind her ear, breaking eye contact.

He opened his mouth, prepared to reply, when the softness drained from her eyes. "At least this operation wasn't a total bust." Her voice returned to the brisk tone of business. "Hope you don't mind committing some lighthearted breaking and entering. Let's get heading to Jared's Auto."

Chapter Eight

By the time Navi pulled up to the side of the road near Jared's Auto, she'd had plenty of time to think — too much time, if she were to be honest. The more she worked alongside Finn, the more her barriers broke down. While she always maintained a level head on the job, that wasn't what threatened her. The way his presence worked under her skin, how he imprinted on her — that endangered the years of careful work she'd done in building impenetrable walls so that the constant goodbyes didn't break her.

Back in the woods, Navi had prepared to deliver the execution like she always did — the hand of justice that had been passed down upon her when the shamans bound the panther spirit to her as a kid. Except Finn had looked her in the eyes like he saw right through the mask she donned and he'd done the job for her. Even now, her heartbeat quickened at the understanding in his eyes, at how he saw to the core of her when so few

Katherine McIntyre

could. Navi scrubbed her face to get herself in the game before hopping out of her car.

As she made her way down the driveway to Jared's Auto, Finn pulled up to the front of the building in that beaut of a Challenger, looking far too gorgeous behind the wheel.

Navi met him out front of the auto shop, soon to become a husk of a building with the owner deceased. The aluminum siding had taken some wear and tear and a couple of the garage doors lining the building were dented and wouldn't shut all the way. The clear glass door of the service section wouldn't deter break-ins for a heartbeat, but if this was a drop site or exchange point, the man probably hadn't been too worried about security.

Already, this night had run on too long, yet there didn't seem to be an end in sight. Even with the temperature drop, the humidity still hung in the air and coated her skin. Navi slunk over to the front door, keeping her pace measured and quiet in case other Landsliders happened to be lurking around here.

She could feel his presence at her back while she fiddled with the knob and damn if her pulse didn't quicken at the lingering scent of leather he brought with him. Her nail turned into a claw as she slipped it in the lock and turned the tumblers until they clicked.

"You take me to the nicest places, Tremere," Finn said behind her, a teasing note in his voice. "What's next? Crack shack in Philly?"

"Like you'd be so lucky," she murmured, trying to restrain her smile while the lock clicked. She opened the door, gesturing inside. Finn winked as he entered, walking in as if he owned the place, a return to the cocky, self-assured guy who'd approached her at the

81

celebration of Dax's victory. Yet the same man had frozen in caves in the grips of some fierce demons. Every time she thought she'd figured him out, he'd rewrite the words to his story, change the sentence mid-read.

She stepped into the auto shop, the smell a familiar one — oil and metal. Navi had spent a fair amount of time under the frame of a car, and any shifter-run auto shops let her play around, given her status as Tribe. Fixing the parts on a car helped her clear her mind in a way talking didn't do, the process of problem-solving something that made sense and gave her the ability to reconcile the issues that didn't. The scent of this place dosed her with comfort even though she remained on the alert for any movement signaling other intruders paying a visit.

Finn strode up to the lone service desk on the far side of the wall, one with a three-tier filing cabinet beside it. Once he'd crouched in front of the cabinet and opened the drawers with a quiet creak and click, he set to rifling through the papers and manila folders inside. Navi trusted him to handle that end of the search, because if the Landsliders were running drugs or fenced goods through here, the other area which might contain evidence would be the garage itself.

She wandered in through the side door, the metallic scent of the auto tools tickling her nose upon entrance. An old Camry sat on joists, the tires removed, while a newer-looking Jetta had the hood popped. Both were barely visible with the faint moonlight trickling in through the slatted windows in the garage doors. Her footsteps echoed through the place, the concrete floors and tall ceilings carrying the shuffling sound with ease. Navi didn't waste time searching with her eyes.

Instead, she sniffed the air, that sense so much sharper even with the conflicting scents of multiple shifters.

The sharp tang of metal, the wet fur of wolves and bears and the robust scent of oil and grease all drew her attention, but nowhere did she pick up the off-scent of meth or any sorts of drugs she was familiar with. However, a sickly-sweet stench did draw her attention, like bug spray on steroids, coming from the stacks of tools and equipment on the wire racks in the back of the garage. Navi slipped in the direction with ease, weaving past the Jetta.

The ratchets and compressors had been left slung about on the shelves in no seeming order, but Navi wasn't looking for them. She ran her fingers over the surfaces while she followed the scent trail, trying to distinguish the source. The cool quiet of the garage seeped through her, amplifying her paranoia. One of the Landsliders could be waiting around any corner. Years of vigilance kept her guard up at all times and she couldn't dismiss how her neck prickled.

Her hand paused over a locked Durabuilt box on the middle shelf. She grabbed the whole thing and set it on the ground before fumbling around on the shelves for the basics. When she rested her hand on a hammer, she returned to the ground and tilted the padlock onto the concrete. Navi slammed the hammer down, breaking the padlock open. The sound reverberated around the room and she glanced at the windows and the door to see if anyone was peering in at her.

Yellow eyes flashed in the garage door windows as someone tried to duck out of sight.

Navi's blood ran cold. She snatched the toolbox from the floor and bolted toward the door. In the same moment, whoever had been watching galvanized to motion. The skitter of their footsteps echoed from outside.

"Finn," she called, her voice tight when she skidded into the main room.

He looked up from behind the desk, his face paler than normal as he clutched a stack of papers.

"We've got company," she growled, whipping around to face the door.

The moment the door flew open, Navi was prepared. On any normal mission with any normal shifter, a simple command could cause them to freeze. However, after the incident at the cave, she didn't trust her ability to work. Instead, when the yellow-eyed bear charged in through the entrance, Navi unleashed a blast of water from her palm.

She funneled her energy into the shove, the wild side of her taking the reins like it did every time she exercised those powers. The element twisted through her, summoned from every drop in the air, every ounce soaked into the earth below her. The jet of water slammed straight into the bear's face. The beast slowed for a second, but even though he had no way of seeing past the spray, he surged again to barrel forward. He rocketed past her, speeding toward the back of the room. Navi bolted for the door, hoping Finn had the common sense to follow.

She darted out right when the bear unleashed an enraged roar and Finn followed seconds later.

"Let's get the hell out of here," he said, already rushing past her for his car. The door had been shoved off the hinges, so she kicked it in front of the entrance before rushing to Finn's Challenger. A curse came from him as she neared.

"Asshole sliced my tires," he spat.

The bear slammed against the flimsy door, sending the thing flying.

"Follow me." Navi raced down the drive toward her Plymouth, parked enough out of the way to avoid backlash. She leapt into the driver's seat of her car, threw the Durabuilt toolbox into the backseat and jammed her key in the ignition. Finn opened the passenger's side of her door and slid inside.

Her engine roared to life.

The bear rushed out from Jared's Auto, heading in their direction. Not like the two of them couldn't take the beast on, but right now, the evidence they'd found in there was paramount and she wasn't about to risk the contents of the Durabilt getting damaged or stolen. She slipped the gear into drive as Finn's door slammed shut. The bear shifter raced toward them, his yellow eyes glowing when he reared up, ready to sink those claws into her car.

Her tires screeched when she jammed her foot on the gas pedal. The car flew forward as she gunned toward the road. She wheeled around, choking billows of gravel and dust coming in through the windows as her car faced the street. Without a second glance to Jared's Auto, she slipped onto the road and accelerated.

Her high-beams sliced through the inky blackness of the country roads while her Plymouth shot down them at double the speed limit. Her heart thudded in her chest, and drops of sweat clung to her forehead. The adrenaline that swilled through her veins crashed down, spreading the silence like a stain in the air between them.

"Bastard scratched up my girl," Finn growled while he stared out of the window. "I hate leaving her there like that."

Navi clutched the wheel a little tighter. "We'll get her back for you tomorrow." His Challenger was a beauty — it had to have been agonizing for him to leave her behind.

"Might have to hold off on that one — as Sierra's beta, I've got duties to attend to and so do you. Or did you forget you guys are presiding over their mating ceremony?" Finn opened the window, letting the breezes gust through her car.

Her skin prickled, but not from the cold. "Ugh, I forgot."

"Try to be a little more disgusted, why don't you?" he teased. She could feel the heat of his gaze on her while she continued to speed down the road, as far and fast away from the auto shop as possible. "Is it the parties involved, or are you one of those anti-love types?"

"Ding, ding, ding," she said, tapping against the side of her steering wheel. The midnight scent of running water and freesia mingling in the breeze swept through her car. "Things like mates are for folks who can afford roots. Not for Tribe." Even when the words escaped her throat, she couldn't help the way her gut twisted. She normally remained in control behind the wheel of her Plymouth, but this conversation teetered into dark, dangerous territory, a yawning maw that threatened to swallow her alive.

"You're telling me no one in the Tribe has ever found a mate? That's hard to believe," Finn said, his voice heated in a way she couldn't dismiss.

"Why the hell do you care?" she shot back, driving past the familiar sight of Beaver Tavern. "It's not like my issues are your problem. And you've got enough problems of your own." She'd been heading for her motel on autopilot, despite the fact that she needed to drop him off somewhere.

"Oh yeah, fuck me for giving a damn about you," he retorted, a familiar anger burning behind his words. "Do you honestly think you were put on this earth to be alone the rest of your life? That your position as Tribe makes you impossible to love?"

Navi's nails turned to claws as they dug into the steering wheel. She pulled over to the side of the road with a screech and slammed the car into Park. Her heart pounded so ferociously she could feel it pulse through her whole body, could hear the sound over and over again. Finn Kelly had the unique way of driving through to her truth every single time, to the point that he wielded the power to devastate her.

The moment those words left him, she wasn't the hardened warrior she'd become, the cool and impartial judge who wandered from town to town. No, she was six years old again and wondering why her parents had given her up. Wondering why every friendship she made fell to pieces. Why she set off for yet another new location each time, leaving everything she'd tried to build behind.

The silence between them was weighed down with all the things they didn't say, but she couldn't be here in this car with him as his larger than life presence threatened to overwhelm. As his words pierced right through to the core of her. Navi might be one of the most powerful individuals on the East Coast, yet this Red Rock beta managed to bring her to her knees with a couple of words.

She slipped out of her car, shutting the door as she stalked in front to the hood and found a spot to lean. On these country roads, few cars would be heading their way at this time of night. She gulped the cool air, willing it to clear her head and soothe the ferocious ache in her chest, a chasm that widened by the second.

A moment later the other door slammed as Finn hopped out from her Plymouth and came to join her. The man was relentless.

"I'm not sorry for giving a fuck about you, Navi," he said, crossing his arms in front of his chest. He leaned against the side of the car, close enough that she could feel the heat emanating off his body. "You've got strength in spades, but there's so much more to you than the burden you're shouldering, sweetheart. I'm more interested in the woman standing before me whose single moment of softness is worth a thousand from anyone else."

She opened her mouth, but the words dried on her tongue. The intensity sparking in Finn's dark eyes, the taut muscles of his neck as he argued with her and how his thick brows furrowed with the same irritation flowing through her — all of it ensnared her. He was supposed to be the same as all the others, a no-strings-attached fling. And yet the more she got to know Finn Kelly, the more she connected with him, fought with him and talked with him, she couldn't help but like the bastard.

The air between them grew thick in her silence. She couldn't convey how the man punched right through her chest to reach a hand out to the little girl who'd never been able to keep a friend. The tug Navi felt for him went beyond carnal to something deeper, stronger and more insidious than she'd first realized. Around him, she couldn't help the way her pulse quickened, or how her guard came down when she rarely allowed anyone in apart from Jess and Lucas.

Finn reached forward, crossing the distance between them as he slid his palm to her face, tilting her chin until their eyes met. The warmth in his gaze as he looked at her and the serious press of those lips near took her breath away, made her forget rules and reason. His touch brought her desire to life, the surge of adrenaline rushing through her before pooling at her core. Her panther lunged for him even as Navi held back. Her wilder side had accepted him the moment they'd first hooked up, but she couldn't just shed her hesitations.

Still, one more taste can't hurt.

She leaned up at the same moment Finn descended. Their lips crushed together with all the passion burning in her chest, the irritation and frustration that threatened to choke her. His one hand wrapped around her waist, the other gripping the nape of her neck with a possessive hold she couldn't help but melt into. Unlike so many others, she could spit venom and he'd go toe to toe with her despite the immense power she had over him.

She slipped her tongue into his mouth, eliciting a groan from him as he tugged her body against his. The thick length of his erection brushed against her inner thigh, igniting her libido. Her panther let out a low purr reverberating through her throat when he kissed her over and over again, her mouth, her neck, her collarbone. She sank into the heat of him, the inferno that threatened to tear her apart and remake her from inside out. If they continued on like this, clothes were going by the wayside and she was liable to fuck him here and now on the side of the road.

He pressed her against the car, bracing her with his big body there as she leaned against the Plymouth, surrendering to the thrill of his skillful mouth on hers, his teeth on her skin.

Headlights came into view from the curve of the road, drawing her attention. A horn blared as a car breezed by, swerving to avoid them. The distraction jarred her out of the haze of just how damn good his lips felt on hers. She didn't have time to be messing around, not now.

Navi pulled away from Finn, from the heat of his embrace and the comfort he offered. Even though her body still revved from the taste of his lips and the way they'd crashed together, her mind took the wheel. They had evidence in the car, a mating ceremony to attend in the morning and she had a set of rules to uphold. Because she'd learned this lesson from an early age. The more she got attached, the more it hurt when she had to leave.

"I've got to get this evidence somewhere safe. I can drop you off along the way," she murmured, hopping in the driver's seat without a second glance. He slipped in on the other side and she set off down the road, trying to ignore how her heart sped in his presence. Trying to forget how he made her yearn.

Chapter Nine

After the day Finn'd had, sleep would be a long time coming.

Navi had peeled away after dropping him off, as though she couldn't escape fast enough. The demons haunting that woman were some fierce and furious ones. He slipped his hands into his pockets when he walked up the short driveway to the cheap apartment he rented, one of the concessions he'd made in order to afford his gym. The papers he'd rifled through at the auto shop had left him with the lingering irritation that he knew Dale Rossi from somewhere, somewhere he couldn't place.

As he walked up the asphalt, a familiar scent caught his attention.

"Waiting up for me, Streaky?" Finn called out to Jer, his nickname well traveled through the pack. "Well, isn't that just darling." As he approached the stoop, Jer sat on the front step with a slight hunch to his shoulders. He leaned over his knees, his tousled chestnut hair obscuring his gaze. Not as if the sight was an unfamiliar one. Jer lived walking distance away, and they'd spent too many years riding out late in the night and stirring up trouble.

Except, Jer's silence unsettled him. His eyes gleamed with his wolf when he looked up.

Finn's stomach tightened.

Jer rose from his perch, a serious look on his mug. "I'm going to need some straight answers from you," he said, tension emanating off him.

Finn restrained the groan that threatened to rip from his throat. He'd had enough of the emotional bullshit today between arguing with Raven and Navi — the last thing he needed was to get flack from one of his best friends, too.

"What's eating you up, brother?" he asked, slumping to the porch steps where Jer now stood. His legs ached, his mind burned with the events of the day, and he wanted a stiff glass of whiskey — not an interrogation.

"I'm done sitting by and watching while you fuck around with Raven," Jer growled, the sound carrying through the late-night air.

"Didn't know you liked to watch," Finn shot back, not in the mood for getting reamed out when Raven's relationship with him wasn't Jer's business in the first place. The pretty boy pack lawyer had flashed those long lashes and that charmer's smile to bring most of the females in the pack to his bedroom and he brought home new conquests every week. He had no room to talk. "Next time I'll leave the bedroom door open."

Jer's eyes flashed and his claws protruded. Finn glared at his friend, not willing to budge on this one. Neither of them claimed patience as a virtue, but for all the times they'd come to blows, they'd always been able to wrangle their shit out.

"You've been leading her on for so damn long and now the whole pack has to watch you drag her through hell again while you chase after this chick from the Tribe?" Jer turned to him, the accusatory tone in his voice spelling out everything.

"Don't go speaking on shit you know nothing about," Finn growled, digging his claws into the wooden planks of his porch. "Even if I want to cut Rae loose, the situation's not so simple. The girl's been hurting for far too long and patching her life in all the wrong ways. You care so much, then instead of jawing off at me, maybe you should try talking to her."

The fight sputtered out of Jer as he sheathed his claws before running his fingers through his chestnut locks. "I don't know how to help her, Finn. She's been in love with you for as long as anyone can remember. If you can't break the cycle, what the hell are we supposed to do?"

He sympathized. The helplessness and the guilt were why he'd been stuck in this spin cycle for far too long. Both of them loved Rae to pieces, but he'd never felt any spark. He sure as hell hadn't felt the maelstrom of emotions that whipped around him every time he was with Navi. Both he and his wolf were growing more attached by the day, to the point where he wasn't sure how the hell he would handle the eventuality of her leaving.

"She wants this fiction that's never going to happen. Like I'll change my stride and fall madly in love with her. I just don't feel it, Jer. I never have, but when we started hooking up we were both too fucked in the head to break it off when we should have." Finn scrubbed his face, relief saturating him at airing this shit with his oldest friend. Sierra had pushed him for answers on occasion with the Raven thing and most of the pack threw in their own jibes, but no one had ever forced the whole story. They understood that when they did, the flimsy strings holding him and Raven together would snap.

"What are you doing chasing around Navi?" Jer asked, curiosity sparking those hazel eyes when he took a seat next to him. "You're going to ruin my rep as the pack slut if you start dipping into every female who enters our territory."

"Please, we both know my winning personality would send the women running in the other direction, fast. Plus, I couldn't manage slicking down a pretty-boy mop like yours." Finn snorted. Navi wasn't a subject he was ready to broach, not with the way she'd worked her way in deeper than comfortable.

"Gosh, golly, you think I'm pretty?" Jer fanned himself before tugging the hand-rolled joint he had tucked behind his ear. He grabbed his Bic and lit it, sending the familiar earthy scent tumbling through the air.

Finn gestured with his hand. "Pass that shit over here. You owe me after storming the gates to my castle. Disrupting my peaceable night."

Jer shook his head as he let out a stream of smoke and passed over the joint. "Cocky fucker. Rae's my girl. I just don't want to see the hurt on her beautiful face anymore." The troubled look in Jer's eyes made him wonder with the way the guy's brows drew together in a concern that Finn had always questioned. Not like Jer made anything clear. The pack lawyer chased after any bit of tail who wandered his way—though Finn had buried himself in denial long enough that he understood.

Finn leaned back, taking a hit off the joint. The moment it touched his lips, he could feel his nerves calming while the smoke filtered up to disappear into the night sky. "If I could take the pain from her, I would. But I'm never going to be her solution, Jer." He looked up to the moon above, visited by a boldness he hadn't felt in those caves — one he hadn't felt in a long time. "Hell, I don't even know if I'll be here forever — my wolf's been begging to run free for far too long."

Jer's fist landed on his arm with a thump. "Stop with that nonsense. You're our beta and, if you ditch, I won't hesitate to find every angle in the book to legally keep you here."

Finn shook his head, taking another hit off the joint as he tried to hide his smirk. The Red Rocks, they'd always been good to him, always would. Despite the restlessness roving through his veins, these were his people — his family.

* * * *

Finn knocked on the door to Sierra's cabin bright and early. Much to Dax's chagrin, she'd requested her beta to drive her to the ceremony in the morning, a compromise since the Tribe was officiating it in the heart of Silver Springs territory. Fitting that the area that Dax had bled for his pack a month earlier would become the spot where they would honor their bond. Finn counted himself lucky to get a few minutes alone with his pack alpha. Ever since she'd met her mate, Sierra spent every spare second getting down and dirty with Dax.

The door creaked open and Sierra stepped into view.

The Red Rock alpha had always been a beauty in the snap-your-neck way, but this must've been the first time he'd ever seen her in a dress. The effect was staggering. The russet red of the curve-hugging floor-length dress she wore accentuated the bronze color of her skin, enhancing the dark waterfall of hair that cascaded down her back. She wore gold bracelets around her wrists, and dark brown, strappy sandals elevated her height until she almost stood toe-to-toe with him.

Finn let out a low wolf-whistle. "Slink into that sort of get-up for me?"

Sierra fixed him with one of her patented death glares. "Start that nonsense and I'll let Dax gut you myself. You know the fact you're bringing me there has him riled." His alpha emanated a brisk, no-nonsense attitude at all times, but she'd met her match with the mountain lion alpha. It had taken one of the most irritating men on the planet to rein in Sierra Kanoska, but when they'd come together, the pair of them were the sort of formidable that threatened to dominate not only the region, but the whole East Coast.

In the face of that power, no wonder he'd been feeling like he was watching from the other side of the glass. Sierra didn't need him to lean on as her beta anymore, not now that she had Dax by her side. Despite the overwhelming happiness he felt for his friend at finding her mate, he couldn't help the sense of displacement that hollowed him, the loss he couldn't shake. However, in asking her to represent the pack by her side today, she'd honored him here and now.

"Ready to go meet your mate?" he asked, extending an arm. "I know I promised a ride in the Challenger, but you'll have to make do with this rental Civic." Even being without his car for a day had been too long, and he itched to have his Challenger back. Navi had arranged the tow and repair courtesy of the Tribe, since it had gotten messed up while on their business.

Sierra lifted a brow while she accepted his arm and together they walked out of her house. "Do I want to know?"

"Casualty on the hunt with Navi for the Landsliders," he said, opening the door for her, the one time his alpha would accept the whole gentleman schtick. "Thanks for recommending me. It's been a nonstop thrill ride." He slipped into the driver's seat, revved the ignition and set off down the road. Sierra leaned against the side, watching the trees flash by along the highway.

"Care to explain what's going on between you and our resident Tribe member?" Sierra asked, her voice sharpening. "I happened to run into Raven at the bar yesterday—she was having a cry in the back room."

Finn resisted the urge to bash his head against the steering wheel. Like always around here, everyone put their noses in each other's business. The criticism weighed down her tone like usual when Sierra butted into their relationship. She viewed the world in black and white and her brain couldn't wrap around the Ouroboros relationship he and Raven had, a toxic cycle neither could break free from.

He pushed on the gas pedal, focusing on the road ahead. Finn swallowed the angry words that sprang to his tongue—riling up the alpha on her mating day wouldn't be the best plan. Even if she was the one picking the fights.

"Raven's going to have to get the hell over me," he said, his words coming out in a growl regardless. "I've told her before and I'll tell her again—my feelings aren't going to somehow change. We've both got to find a better way to process our damage."

Sierra turned toward him—he could feel her patented alpha stare coming down hard. "What's going on with her?"

Finn shook his head. "Not my place to say, boss. We owe you our loyalty, not our pasts. Some memories are too painful to unearth."

Sierra's lips pressed tight together, and as he glanced in her direction, the look in her dark eyes conveyed far too much understanding. He'd always known Sierra had her own demons to chase. They all did.

"As long as I don't lose my beta to the Tribe, your business is your own," she murmured, conceding the fight. "I don't know what I'd do without you to call me on my shit, Finn." Sierra rummaged through his glove box, causing the familiar rustle of plastic packaging as she found his emergency smokes. Finn one-handed the steering wheel, plucking the box from her hands.

"No way am I going to be responsible for Dax breaking my neck because you showed up to your mating ceremony smelling like a chimney." He tossed the pack into his backseat amidst her complaints. Even with the temporary distraction, her statement shot through to the heart of him. The conflict brewing in his chest threatened to spill over, those words poised on his lips. Except, Sierra had traveled miles away from her bad situation to find a home and her place in life. She wouldn't understand the divide deepening in him by the day, the fear of leaving the place he loved and the urge to wander that gripped him by the throat.

"I'm the alpha," Sierra shot back. "If I want to show up smelling like a chimney or even a dung heap, that's my prerogative."

"It sure is," he responded, not bothering to hide the smile that stole over his face. Despite her arguments, she wasn't making any leaps for the pack in the backseat. Sierra might be a stubborn sonofabitch, but she had the most level head out of anyone he knew. The Red Rock pack couldn't be in better hands with a leader like her.

"So, honesty time," she said, staring at her hands. "I know Dax and I already bit the bonded bullet, but have you kept a pulse on how the pack feels about this transition? I know you'll always be straight with me."

"The pack couldn't be more stable," Finn said without hesitation. "The trials Dax went through to solidify his leadership plus the way both packs banded together during the attacks made it pretty clear what a good team the two of you make. Your union is only going to strengthen the Red Rocks and the Silver Spring packs."

Today wasn't for mentioning how their union had become so strong Sierra no longer needed him as beta, even if she hadn't realized the transition yet. Working alongside Navi to bust this smuggling ring had provided a breath of fresh air, and Finn couldn't lie to himself — when the Tribe moved on from this area, his future here would be blank, erased. Like the sense of purpose he'd once clung to had departed with the changes.

Sierra's hands curled into her dress, but an air of resolve radiated around her, one matching the confidence of her stance and the steadiness of those dark eyes. Dax was one lucky bastard, because Sierra possessed a shade of loyal that rarely existed nowadays. "Thanks. You're a good one, Finn. Even if Raven doesn't end up being your mate, I hope to be attending one of these ceremonies for you down the line."

Her words slugged him in the gut with an intense longing, one he couldn't even hope to explain. He'd wanted the path she was preparing to embark on for so long, a forever commitment and a family of his own, but no one among the Red Rocks or in this region clicked with him like he hoped. And hell, he knew what a difficult bastard he was to deal with in the first place. The bond between Sierra and Dax, the depth of their relationship and the way they helped each other rise from their pasts—he wanted that with an intensity bordering on desperation.

They pulled up to the clearing, which had been transformed over the past couple of days for the ceremony. The beaten dirt circle Dax fought in remained there and the large lake glittered in the distance, but dozens of chairs had been brought out to fill the clearing and a wire archway was placed in the front and woven with lilies. Already, most of the pack had taken their seats and more than a couple of Tribe members were millng around the clearing. The air buzzed with tension, the same sort that infiltrated before a wedding. Unlike those celebrations, though, mating ceremonies involved a level of magic to the commitment, honoring the origin of their abilities and the source of their power.

Finn pulled the car into Park and turned to face Sierra. "Ready to go meet your mate?" he asked.

"The better question is if he's ready for me." She flashed him a grin, the expression on her face radiant.

Today, Sierra of the Red Rocks would be bonded to her mate in the eyes of the Tribe and, despite Finn's own damage, he couldn't be happier.

Chapter Ten

Navi fidgeted in her dress, already feeling uncomfortable. The sunshine was out in full force and gentle breezes brought traces of honeysuckle through the clearing, causing the lake behind them to ripple every once in a while. Sierra and Dax couldn't have asked for a more beautiful day for their ceremony. She'd presided over dozens of these before and, without a doubt, the more touching and perfect the ceremony, the more she wanted to gag.

Jess crouched in her champagne dress, preparing the incense that would be burning during the ritual. Fires leapt high in the ornate pit they'd set up, one they transported with them on the road. The heat nearby amplified the summer's hold and sweat pricked her brow, beads of it sliding down her cheek. Dax was dressed sharper than normal with a charcoal vest and black slacks, but he'd opened up the top buttons of his white shirt and he wore a pair of boots with the ensemble. The man looked gorgeous while he paced back and forth around the clearing.

However, only one guy as of late had the ability to knock the breath from her.

The click of a door opening drew more than just her attention. Dax near jumped from where he stood when the rental car pulled into the lot. Sierra Kanoska stepped out of the passenger side, and every gaze zeroed in on the woman. Her Native American heritage shone under this sun between the bronzed skin her dress exposed, the elegant cheekbones and her raven-wing hair. The woman radiated confidence, an unshakable power that left no one questioning who was in charge.

Sierra wasn't the reason Navi smoothed down the fabric of her knee-length azure dress. Finn stepped out of the driver's side, and she couldn't help how her pulse quickened at the sight of him. The pale blue button-down he wore provided the perfect contrast to his corded, tan skin and his khakis couldn't hide the thick muscles of his legs. The moment his dark eyes landed on her, she forgot what she was doing and why she was even here.

An elbow nudged her in the side, drawing her attention front and center.

"Might want to close your mouth," Jess whispered in her ear. "You're drooling."

Navi shot a glare, crossing her arms over her chest. "Sierra dressed up, that's all," she said. "I was surprised."

Jess snorted as she straightened next to her. "Then how come your gaze was focused on the Red Rock beta?" Damn the woman. Jess knew Navi far too well. She sucked in a deep breath, pinching the claw pendant between her breasts. The roadside makeout session with Finn had been a terrible idea and she didn't know how to quit him, not while they worked this case together. Not with him looking at her like she was the only thing that existed on the planet.

Navi fought the shiver rolling down her spine under the strength of his gaze.

Dax approached where they stood, his focus on his advancing mate. The man normally exuded cockiness, but the Red Rock alpha had discovered the way to cut him off at the knees. Lucas strolled up to Navi's other side, his big presence casting a shadow over her. Since he stood at least a foot over her, he always loomed, but she'd never once found herself intimidated—the guy pulled to the side of the road every time he spotted roadkill he might be able to save.

"Ready to unite yet another fated match?" Lucas asked, clapping a hand on her shoulder. "I know this part's your favorite."

Navi shot him a dirty look right when Jess piped up. "I think she's reconsidering her avid anti-love status with the longing looks she keeps swapping with a certain wolf."

Hearing it out loud caused all those fears and worries percolating around to coil tight within her and her hands balled into fists on instinct, the claws digging into her palms. Navi fought to keep her temper level, tamping down the urge to start slinging punches. "I think today's a great reminder of how fleeting love is for us, and you know it. They've got a home, a family. We're Tribe. We get the road—no attachments. No commitments."

Jess zipped her mouth at that, her lips pressing tight together, and Lucas squeezed Navi's shoulder in response. Even though she wasn't able to keep her bitterness at bay, she didn't worry about the others understanding—they knew the life sentence they'd been handed.

Navi stepped in front of the pyre and lifted her arms to the crowd. "Dax Williams and Sierra Kanoska, approach," she called. Her voice echoed through the clearing as a hush descended. Dax grabbed Sierra's hand while they both approached, despite the exasperated glance Sierra shot him at the public display. Like the whole mating ceremony wasn't in front of both their packs.

Finn made his way to the front of the crowd, his hands slipped into his pockets while he watched. She could feel his gaze on her even as she focused on the two approaching. The demand in his dark eyes was one she could never acquiesce to, the hope flickering there one she would crush. In Finn Kelly's eyes, she saw dreams of a future, one they'd never have.

"We are here today to witness the mating of Dax, alpha of the Silver Springs pack, and Sierra of the Red Rock pack. Through the Tribe, the spirits above will descend to honor this union." At her words, she could feel her power ignite within her, the ancient spirit of her panther stirring in her chest. The heady scent of the incense grew stronger, the flames turning shades of green and purple as it burned. The tribal tattoos weaving up her arms and legs heated, the way the lines sometimes did when she used her power. Navi breathed in the spice and bathed in the heat of the fire, letting the flames heighten her awareness.

The shaman's incense sparked the feral part of her, the soul she'd been bonded with, and she wasn't the only one afflicted. Jess and Lucas responded in kind, their eyes glowing with the fury of their beasts simmering beneath the surface.

She sucked in a deep breath when she approached Dax and Sierra who stood beside each other, facing her. Not like Jess and Lucas couldn't be the speaker, but they tended to drag ceremonies out way too long. Navi preferred to cut to the quick of this nonsense.

"Our ancestors were forged by the elements — earth, wind, fire and water. These mighty creatures roamed the land, connected to humans by the ancient magic of the shamans. In that spirit, we are bound together by the tethers of pack, of Tribe, but even deeper and more permanent is the mating bond." Navi's stomach flipped as she reached the next part. Even though everyone focused on the happily mated couple, Finn's gaze hadn't left her. She couldn't forget his words from the night before — she had the feeling she'd be carrying them with her for a long time on the lonely road ahead.

"Your mate is the other half of your foundation, your source of strength when you feel weak. Together, you are strong. You are complete in the eyes of your pack, in the eyes of your Tribe and, most importantly, in the eyes of each other." Navi's voice rang out through the clearing.

Sierra's small smile and the way her eyes softened when she looked at Dax transformed her features. He beamed with a sunlit strength back at her. Navi's heart wrung like a wet rag, the too familiar bitterness descending. Yet again, she stood witness to a happiness she'd never have, a union and community she would never be a part of. Hell if these ceremonies didn't strip her down like turpentine, year after empty year.

Navi closed her eyes, summoning her panther like nudging a part of her to life. She reached out with both hands and Lucas and Jess grabbed hers. With the three of them connected, she could feel the growing power of their Tribe flow through her, the swell of the ruling force they'd been granted from birth.

"Sierra Kanoska," Navi intoned, her words coming out cold and unearthly while she floated away on the tides of the power rushing through her. "Dax Williams. Do you acknowledge the bond between you in the presence of the spirits?"

"I do," Sierra said, her voice ringing out strong and clear.

"As do I," Dax followed, his tone wry yet warm.

Navi squeezed Jess' slim hand and Lucas' coarse one as the strength swelled within her, the very molecules vibrating from the sheer force of their connection, like standing in hurricane winds. "The spirits bless your mating. May you navigate this lifetime together." The words left her lips and the panther took over, a howl ripping from her throat. The sound grew raw, furious and demanding as it echoed through the clearing, joined by Jess' and Lucas' beasts.

In these moments, she wasn't Navi Tremere anymore—she was something ancient, something primal and something more than she could imagine as her human self. The panther attached to her had traveled along many lifetimes, from one Tribe member to another, but the immensity of the knowledge the spirit had collected along the way was too much to comprehend. She dipped her toe into the power on a regular basis, but moments like these, she plunged straight into the pool.

The sound faded as their howls came to a close and her throat throbbed in the aftermath. Silence reigned throughout the clearing for a single, solemn moment.

Until, one by one, each shifter standing before them lifted their heads and returned the howls. Their voices pierced the air, the animalistic sound reverberating through her very bones. The earth beneath her feet became alive, from the wind sweeping strands of her hair to the splash of the lake's water lapping to the shore and the crackle of the fire behind her.

Dax grabbed Sierra by the waist and planted a kiss on her lips, breaking the formality of the moment. She sank into his embrace and the howls quieted, replaced by catcalls and cheers. Navi tilted her head in silent acknowledgment. The ceremony was over and now the celebrations would begin.

* * * *

As the Silver Springs and Red Rock packs set to partying, music blared over the speakers they'd set up, pulsing through the clearing. Picnic tables had been wrangled into place early this morning, every ounce of the surfaces covered by a buffet of grilled chicken, roasted pork, dripping ribs and whatever sides the prep crew had thrown in. With all these shifters in one locale, the top item on the menu would be red meat, as rare as they could make it.

Standing outside the rustic Silver Springs' cabin, Navi couldn't shake the sense of déjà vu. Not a month ago, she had joined them in celebration after Dax had won the fight against his brother and they had been breaking out the ale together then, sharing in the excitement of his win after the trials both packs had been through. A certain pack beta had been a relentless flirt for her attention that night, too.

Navi took a seat at one of the empty picnic tables, tipping back the bottle of Yuengling she'd nabbed from the cooler. The beads of condensation imprinted on her palm, a coolness against the heat radiating from the midday sun. She didn't even need to turn around to sense him there behind her.

"I told you and I meant it back then — that was a one-time thing," she said, leaning against the picnic table and resting her forearm on the weathered surface.

Finn settled onto the bench beside her, his weight causing the planks to creak. "And last night was...?" he asked, his brow lifted. This close, she could smell the leather on him even now, the fresh-cut grass as if he'd rolled in it. Her panther preened at the scent, not helping to quell the attraction flushing through her body.

"Last night was a lapse in judgment," Navi drawled, soaking in the sunshine. She glanced to a gaggle of Red Rocks laughing and hanging out a couple of tables over. Except one of them wasn't laughing at all and the woman zeroed her laser gaze in on Navi. *Spirits be damned.* Raven watched her with an intensity reserved for competition, a fight Navi wanted no part of. "A mistake I'm surer of with every second," she said. "Looks like your girlfriend isn't keen on sharing, either."

Finn's gaze followed hers, and his chicory eyes darkened. "I made my stance with her clear," he said, radiating irritation while he tipped back his bottle of beer. "Not my problem if she refuses to accept we don't amount to anything."

Navi shrugged, feigning indifference despite the way her chest burned. "Don't know why you're telling me.

Figured I'd give you the heads-up since you're the one who'll be stuck dealing with the mess."

Finn turned toward her, his big body casting an even larger shadow. "You're still clinging to that bullshit?" he asked, as brazen as ever. His gaze flashed with the audacity few dared to pull around her. After seeing her in Tribe capacity with all the unrestrained power rushing through, he should've been steering clear — Jess and Lucas didn't have a throng of people by their side. However, as always, Finn seemed completely unafraid. He might freeze in caves or tight spaces, but, unlike so many, he treated her like an equal.

Navi took another swig from her bottle, trying to dispel the prickle that traveled her arms at the territory they were sailing into. The bastard had an uncanny way of driving straight through her avoidance tactics. She cast another glance in Raven's direction — nope, the woman hadn't stopped glaring. *Joy.* The exact sort of complication she avoided on principle. Finn watched her, too, those brown eyes curious despite his curt tone. Even with the sun beating down on her, cold suffused her insides.

"I'm clinging to 'that bullshit' because it's all I have," she murmured, the words coming out quieter than intended. She picked at the label of her bottle, refusing to look at Finn. "You might have the luxury of expressing your affection — you've got a family here, a pack, a home. You don't understand what it's like to make connections and lose them over and over again. Eventually, you stop, because you know the outcome — you've lived that pain too many times." Her throat tightened and she stopped, not willing to go on.

An arm slipped around her shoulders, his warmth flooding through her. Navi squeezed tight to the bench, digging her nails into the underside of the wooden planks. Finn pulled her to him and, even though she should've resisted, should've stepped away, she couldn't help but fall into the blissful heat of his embrace. He gave his affection and his touch like those motions cost him nothing, like each effort to reach out didn't scrape a bit more of his psyche.

"If I'm so fulfilled here," he murmured, his breath warm against her ear, "then why the hell can't my wolf settle? Why the fuck, on the day of my alpha's mating ceremony, do I feel like everything I've built here is slipping away from me?" He tightened his grip around her arm, the signal she needed to understand these words were for her alone. That despite the aspects of him seeming like an open book, he didn't offer every page.

Navi looked at him and when their eyes met, she saw him—truly saw him. The slight bags under his eyes from lack of sleep, the troubled press of his mouth. He was so loud, so vibrant and so quick to feel that few would see the hesitation beneath the surface. Even she'd missed it, so focused on trying to fight the way he made her feel too intensely every time she was around him.

His jaw tightened and he reached for his beer, taking a swig. As he relaxed his grip on her, she extricated herself and adjusted to face him. The bumping beat of whatever rock song the packs were blasting echoed through the clearing along with several cheers and screams as Dax and Sierra took to dancing amidst their packs. The Red Rock alpha might not be the showy sort, but her partner could make up for that in spades. A distance spread between them with the silence, one she couldn't let settle.

Navi lifted her bottle. "Well, then, it sounds like we're both fucked."

His mouth quirked and he clinked his beer to hers. "If that's what you want, darling, I've been waiting to peel the dress off you from the moment I pulled into this lot." The heat in his voice burned hotter than the August sun and Navi's core clenched tight at his words. He scanned her with a predator's intensity, his wolf clear in his eyes.

The first time was just a fling, but in the interim, this mess had developed, the sort Navi tended to run screaming from. Finn Kelly came with complications like his ex-fuck buddy and he was also tethered to this place, a beta in the Red Rock pack. Even still, she couldn't help the comfort she felt in his arms and couldn't deny the sparks that flew between them every time their eyes met. However, as much as her body reacted to him and the sight of him there wearing a cocky smirk and fancy clothes begging to be crumpled drove her wild, she couldn't indulge.

If they hooked up again, this time their collision would be real. It would mean more to her than a no-strings one-night stand and tap into feelings she hadn't allowed for herself in far too long. And that meant it would ruin her all the more when she left.

Chapter Eleven

As the night wore on and the packs continued to celebrate, Finn ended up buzzed, horny and frustrated.

He leaned against the side of the cabin and lobbed another empty bottle in the over-full trashcan. No matter how many Yuenglings he tipped back, he couldn't get the gorgeous Tribe member off his mind. She'd ditched a little bit ago with Jess and Lucas, because the packs weren't cutting completely loose with them around. Not everyone disregarded authority like he did and the East Coast Tribe ranked at the top of the ladder. Until they'd talked, he'd never considered how lonely her life on the road was. How she must feel to have everyone treat her as different because of how she'd been born.

This whole night stirred up far too many emotions, the sort he strayed from at all costs. Life was better when he stepped into the studio, laying punches into the bag with singular focus he couldn't find elsewhere.

A piercing howl rang through the clearing, one he recognized at once from his alpha. Every eye zoned in on her while she stood on one of the picnic tables, her raven hair streaming behind her back with the gentle breeze that slipped by.

"Tonight I want to honor those who couldn't be here—Greg and Seamus." Sierra's voice carried through the clearing and a hush fell at the mention.

Dax hopped on the picnic table beside her and lifted his beer. "Raise a glass," he called out, his strength as radiant as hers. "We toast tonight to the pack we have now and those who have fallen. All of you are recognized—all of you are what makes us strong."

Finn lifted his glass like everyone else and the following howl lifted the hairs on his arms. The sound was familiar, of home and pack. The thought dosed him with guilt after what he'd admitted to Navi earlier, but around her, he didn't have to pretend. When he stood by her side, he was raw, real and unashamedly himself—no lies.

The soft tread of footsteps alerted him to a newcomer and those familiar winsome eyes held all the sadness to bring his self-loathing to the forefront. He'd been as clear as he could with Raven, but he wasn't sure if she would ever be able to let him go—not fully. Finn reached down to the table but groped air. He'd already tossed his beer.

"Have fun with your Tribe fling?" she asked upon approach. The skirt of her violet swing dress swished around her calves with her movements, the dress fitting her effortless grace.

"Thought we had a conversation," Finn warned, bursting with irritation. "What I do with Navi isn't your business, Rae." She eyed him up with that look, the sultry one that meant she had one thing on the mind, the same pent-up frustration riding his nerves.

"Not like she took you home with her," Raven said, tilting her bottle to her mouth nice and slow as she took a swig.

His wolf itched, too, the need to fuck, to bury himself in someone and unleash the edge driving him in a real way. However, if he caved here with her, Raven would never take his words seriously. Ever since Navi had crashed into his life, he'd wanted more than ever for his word to mean something.

"I'm fine," he bit out, averting his gaze in case she tried to keep pushing.

Rae could read him all too well after their years together and she'd pick up his frustration in a heartbeat. Not like he and Navi had made themselves exclusive or classified the raw emotion brewing between them as anything other than a fling. He didn't give a damn. Finn didn't want anyone else but her. For the first time, distracting himself with Raven held no allure, not compared to how his synapses flared to life in Navi's presence. How she made him long for something real.

"You don't seem fine to me," she murmured before tipping back her bottle again. The way she said the words, he wasn't sure who she referred to—him or herself. He might have his own demons he hid from, but Raven had so many that facing them might unmake her.

As he scanned the party, he caught Jer's gaze, trying to wordlessly will him over. His best friend nodded in response once he caught the vibe of the situation between him and Raven. In less than a minute, Jer sidled over with one of the pack elders, Gene.

"What the hell is Finn Kelly doing hanging around the fringes like some wallflower?" Jer called out, his smile natural and casual, as if he hadn't come to be the much-needed cockblock. "You should be in the middle of that mess, pulling out your wicked dance moves." His eyes twinkled with amusement at his own joke — Finn didn't dance. Not now, not ever.

"I've been watching yours, Jer," Raven responded, crossing her arms over her chest while she leaned against the cabin wall. "The sprinkler's been passé since it was invented. Stick to the bedroom."

Finn snorted. He never got to experience her natural razor wit since she treated him differently from Jer, with that lovesick reverence that he'd come to detest. He missed the time before they began sleeping together, when they'd been friends and their lives were less complicated.

Gene sank into one of the lawn chairs beside him, kicking his feet out and putting a can of Bud in the holder. "The lot of you have too much energy to spare. I exhausted my party days a long time ago."

Finn nudged the metal rim of the chair with his boot. "Come on now, you're still up and hanging with everyone. You're a trooper."

The old man smiled, his wrinkles crinkling as he stared out to the leaping flames of the firepit they'd formed. Gene had been friendly with his parents, one of the few who'd given gave a damn about what happened to their waste-of-space selves. Finn scratched the nape of his neck. In all the chaos of today, he'd never gotten to do more research on the name of Dale Rossi, but he couldn't shake the feeling he knew that name, deep in his marrow.

"Hey, boss," Finn said, kicking the bottom of the chair to get Gene's attention. "Mind if I ask a question?"

Gene's gnarled brows drew together when he looked up, but he heaved a reluctant sigh. "Only if you find a better way of asking. Jostling's not good for these bones." They both knew that was bullshit. As much as he talked the old-and-antiquated talk, the man could sling a mean punch and kept up with them in the sparring ring.

"You ever run into a Dale Rossi?" he asked. Even saying the name out loud sent a chill through him, but the look from Gene that followed dosed his veins with ice.

"Boy, what are you of all people bringing that name up for?" he asked, his tone sharp. Despite the crackle of the fire in the distance and the laughter floating along on the gentle summer breezes, Finn's skin pebbled with goosebumps. The same wrong, wrong feeling rushed through him, but despite the way he fought to remember, those memories stayed buried. He shook his head even as Gene's brows furrowed and he pressed his lips tight.

"The man caused enough problems for your folks." Gene lowered his voice and Finn crouched beside him. Jer and Raven stood beside each other, throwing barbs and feigning inattention, even though he caught the glances the two of them snuck. "Rossi's the bastard who got them hooked on meth in the first place."

Finn swallowed, hard. He'd known the name sounded familiar, but his folks had always called the guy Ace. If he'd dug up pictures, he would've recognized him on the spot. Finn would never forget the man who'd capped his parents after their deal went bad. Ace vanished for a while after the Red Rocks reported him, but Finn shouldn't have been surprised the bastard aligned with the Landsliders.

Finn had spent the last fifteen years trying to expunge the memories of the day from his mind. Of the blood soaking into the floor, staining his feet. Of the dread choking him at the sight of his parents lying there, dead. Finn's relationship with his parents had been complex, but he'd always wished for the chance to see them change. To tell them how much they'd hurt him with their addictions.

"Thanks, Gene," he said, his voice coming out a lot steadier than he expected. If one of the biggest meth dealers in this region was helping the Landsliders, no wonder they managed to stay steps ahead. Tonight, he'd tip back another beer and watch the fire until it died out, but tomorrow, he needed to call Navi first thing.

* * * *

Finn woke to the sound of his phone ringing. He winced a second later when the throbbing descended, the celebration from last night catching up with him. He rolled over to face his clock, the neon-red numbers smacking him in the face with his late-morning wake-up. On any normal day, Finn was up and out by dawn, but, with how late the celebrating had gone on last night and the unrest that had set his nerves on edge, his sleep had been fitful at best.

"Hey," he muttered into the phone, not even bothering to look at the caller ID.

"Rough night, champ?" a teasing voice responded. "Don't tell me you're just getting up now?"

"Okay, I won't," he said, tugging on a pair of clean gym shorts from the laundry pile he never put away. "You calling with news?"

"I'm on my way to pick you up," Navi said. "We've got a shaman to pay a visit to."

"See you soon," he responded, ending the call as he rummaged around the mess of books and rumpled clothes on his floor. He found one of his work shirts and tugged it on. Shifter males always kept more pairs of clothes than the average guy due to the situations where they ripped through pairs of pants or lost a favorite shirt in the middle of an emergency. The carry-a-spare technique worked for most of them, but no one could anticipate every instance they'd need to shift.

By the time he'd brushed his teeth, and slipped into his sneakers, he caught the click of tires outside his place. He might have towed his car, but he needed to check on his Challenger at the shop after how she'd been battered by the asshole outside Jared's Auto. No matter how good the mechanic was, they didn't treat her with the same level of care he did. Still, with the folks he'd encountered involved with the Landsliders, he would be lucky if this was the worst that happened.

Footsteps sounded along the walkway, so Finn grabbed his keys and slipped his wallet into his pocket before making his way to the door. He'd never had the pleasure of meeting a shaman, but if this excursion ended the way the others did, he could burn some of this restless energy with slinging punches and tearing into Landsliders claws first. He opened the door, greeted by knuckles. Navi paused, her hand lifted and ready to knock.

"How is it that you keep getting more gorgeous every time I see you?" he flirted, shutting his door behind him as he joined her outside.

Navi rolled her eyes, launching an idle punch to his biceps. "I've got better uses for your mouth than false flattery," she murmured, the seductive sound of her voice revving his engines in a way no one else could. His cock throbbed, sparking to life at the idea of spreading her legs and taking a taste. A smirk quirked her lips. "You can throw all that talented talk into charming the shaman we're visiting." The glint in her eyes was telltale — she knew what a tease she was being right now.

His flattery wasn't false, though — despite the striking dress she had worn last night, he loved seeing her like this. Right now she wore jeans that hugged those dangerous curves, and a stained wifebeater with a film of sweat pressing it to dusky skin he longed to sink his teeth into. She smelled like sweat, oil and metal, his favorite things, and he breathed the scent in, slinking closer beside her. Navi walked with a power to her stance, a comfortable confidence flowing through every movement.

She hopped into her old Plymouth and he slid into the other side, the car creaking as he sat. This thing was a deathtrap on wheels, making him miss his baby all the more. Navi started the ignition, put her foot on the pedal and they took off down the winding road leading to his apartment.

"How was the rest of the night?" Navi asked. Even though she kept her voice light, she had caught the way Raven had stared at him and the edge in her tone. Finn might be an idiot and a hothead on occasion, but even he could figure this one out.

"I didn't hook up with Raven, if that's what you're asking," he said, a grin quirking his lips.

Navi scowled, but her body remained relaxed in the seat and her grip loose on the steering wheel. "Did those words come out of my mouth? Stop fluffing your ego, Kelly."

He smirked and rolled down the window, letting the breezes flow in through the car. They raced down the highway, farther outside the towns and toward the deeper woods where the pines and oaks cast long shadows. He hadn't known of any shamans living around these parts, but as they were reclusive and a rare breed to begin with, they didn't often make themselves known to shifters or humans. Too many sought their elemental magic and a lot of the shamans ended up dragged into problems beyond their pay grade or used by whoever cornered them first.

"When we confront Rossi, he's mine," Finn said, his words coming out harsher than intended. Saying his name out loud made him want to flinch, his desire for revenge a secret he'd kept for so long. "The Landsliders recruited the biggest dealer this area's seen. He'd been MIA for a while, but based on the information we got the other day, he's back in action."

"Sounds like you've got a personal vendetta against him," Navi said as she turned off the highway down one of the gravel roads that crunched under her tires. "Promise you're not going to bum-rush this scumbag when we get him in our sights?"

His heartbeat picked up and the numbness threatened to descend as he opened his mouth. The words dried there. He wanted to tell her more than anything, but he couldn't force his past out in the open like that.

"Hey," she said, her voice steady as a stone. "I'm not pushing for information here. I just need to know you won't go jumping into any more caves headfirst." The rational side of her was something he appreciated more and more while they worked together. She balanced his hair-trigger emotional responses like no one else could.

Finn tugged out his smokes and lifted the pack. "You mind if I light up?"

She waved him on. He peeled the wrapping off and tossed the plastic out of the window before slipping the cigarette between his lips. The first tug of nicotine was glorious and the exact thing he needed. His wolf thrashed in his chest, desperate to fight or fuck something. He'd been burning pent-up sexual energy after every interaction with Navi, which amped him up way more than normal. On top of that, the discovery of Dale Rossi's return wired him like nothing else.

He sucked in another drag from his cigarette and let the smoke trail out of the window as he buzzed. The words slipped unbidden. "The bastard killed my parents."

The car jerked as Navi's focus slipped from the wheel, her brows furrowing. He clenched his jaw, bracing himself for the coddling or awkward response everyone gave to the poor orphan boy. He hated it. Yet both man and wolf couldn't help the honesty erupting from him around this woman, part of the undeniable way she grounded him.

"Then you'll be the one to kill him," was all she said, a growl to her words and the panther in her eyes. In that moment, the sheer aggression in her stance, the determination in her voice and the way she delivered those words as the solemn truth gave everything he needed right now.

Finn had tried to fall for Raven over years of affection, touch and time, but he knew deep in his gut he'd never brushed the surface of what he should be feeling. However, with Navi, it was no quiet stream or gentle footsteps. He'd fallen for her like the sudden drop off a cliff face, with the fury of the rapids and with the deep awareness that this woman would be branded on his bones for the rest of his life.

Chapter Twelve

Gravel crunched, twigs snapped and rogue branches scraped against her Plymouth as Navi drove deeper into the thick woods in this area, farther and farther away from civilization. Finn's presence dwarfed her car and even with the windows down and the cool night breezes streaming in, she found it hard to breathe. She'd be lying if she claimed she hadn't stayed awake staring at the ceiling and wondering all last night if he'd found his way to Raven's bed.

Navi shouldn't care, since the most she might get with him was one more scorching night. Except the thought of him with someone else twisted her insides to knots and made her panther rage with a ferocity that almost brought her claws out.

"Your Rossi friend's been dabbling with dangerous folks," she murmured, trying to keep her eyes on the road ahead and not drifting to the muscled, gorgeous guy by her side. "The meth I found in the auto shop didn't smell the same—it's been laced with shamanic magic somehow. And my compulsion hasn't been working on the Landsliders. Either the reason is magical, or Mackey's got a hold on them that's trumping our abilities."

"How exactly does that work?" Finn asked, leaning back in his seat with a creak. "You could compel shifters to do your bidding? Seems like an unfair advantage."

Navi's temper simmered. She'd been saddled with this responsibility from a young age, and she'd dealt with the blaze of fear folks looked at her with every time they understood what she could do. No one bothered to try to understand why the Tribe had been given these abilities — why they were necessary to govern. The job was thankless — they came and risked their lives to break up shifter conflicts when needed and, once they'd done their job, most packs wanted them far away as fast as possible.

"Yeah, because we're supposed to regulate you assholes with no weapons to our advantage, nothing but ourselves to combat a bunch of hotheaded beasts ready to maul each other. With the amount of folks who hate our guts, it doesn't matter how powerful we are — one against an entire pack ends poorly." Her Plymouth rolled over bigger stones at this point in the pathway, branches sweeping over the roof of her car. She winced at the scratching sound.

"So you guys use your compulsion like a cop with a gun," Finn said, drumming his fingers along the side of the window. "What do you do about corrupt cops in the system, though?" His gaze pierced her through. Navi pursed her lips, the words stolen. As fast, her irritation deflated in the face of the understanding and empathy Finn offered. In the way he could relate so readily to her and never once backed away in fear.

"They're rare—the spirits are picky about who they bond with. However, in those instances, we hunt the bastard down. Mackey might have once been a comrade, but the second he started down his path of using his abilities for his own selfish exploits, the second he helped the Landsliders to rise, he became the exact nightmare we're meant to protect the shifter populace from."

Up ahead, a cabin came into view, the orange glow of dim lamps emanating from the window.

"Looks like your shaman friend kept the midnight oil burning," Finn murmured, finishing another cigarette. "Did you call to give him the heads-up, or are we busting in on this poor guy's fortress of solitude?"

Navi snorted. "Of course not. Surprise visits mean no time to cover up anything hinky. Shamans might have been our companions all these years, but Mackey has a unique way of turning people to his side."

She pulled her Plymouth into Park. When she stepped out of her car, the mystical energy swept over her with a thick stickiness in the air worse than the late summer humidity. Shifters had a special connection with shamans, having been created by those ancient magic users. With the Tribe, doubly so. Rich incense hung heavy in the stagnant air and the oily taste of magic with every breath made her nerves buzz with awareness.

Finn's eyes gleamed amber, his wolf showing. "Holy fuck. This place is loaded with power."

Navi hid her grin. "Have you ever been around shamans before?" she asked, leading the way toward a front door covered by painted chalk-white symbols.

Animal skulls rested on the railings of the porch, bleached over time. Patches of flowers, thick leaves and tall grasses bloomed all around the perimeter of the cabin. Navi didn't have to guess every plant in the bunch could be used for something. Shamans utilized nature's tools to perform their magic, and herbs were an intrinsic part of their rituals.

"Nope," he responded. "You're about to pop my shaman cherry." Finn stepped up behind her, his shadow stretching past and his presence making her body spark with awareness. No matter how much she tried to argue with herself, the electricity between them was undeniable.

"You've got quite a way with words, country boy," she drawled before stepping to the door and knocking. Floorboards creaked from inside as footsteps followed.

The door swung open and a middle-aged man dressed in a pressed button-down and black slacks stepped into view. The tan skin, dark eyes and wide jawline emphasized his Tibetan heritage. With his slicked-back hair and the expensive cologne drowning out the incense, Joe Ganzorig didn't fit the profile of the other shamans she'd met, ones committed to a more naturalistic, esoteric lifestyle.

"What do you want?" he asked, his tone sharp while he glanced between the two of them. His gaze rested on Navi and he took a step back as if he'd figured who she was.

"Ganzorig?" Navi took command, knowing her status as Tribe opened doors in a way the average shifter never could. She stuck her hand out. "I'm Navi Tremere of the East Coast Tribe. There have been some incidents in the area as of late and I've got a couple of questions for you."

He reached out and shook her hand, even while his eyes narrowed in caution. Whether the man had anything to do with the altered meth, one thing became clear—he didn't like others encroaching on his space. Too bad for him, because Navi needed answers. Rossi lurked somewhere in this area, but until she found a lead, they'd be wasting time chasing rumors and fires like before.

"Come on in," he said, stepping away from the entrance so they could enter. Even with the caution in his stance, Navi didn't sense a shift in the power dominating the air. If he was readying an attack, her panther would be the first on alert.

Based on the painted runes and small animal bones decorating the exterior of the house, Navi expected more of the same on the inside. The shamans she'd visited before fell squarely in the hippie category and their houses reflected the bones, herbs and dust sort of magic they practiced. Not this guy.

His modern interior of black cabinetry, silver hardware, leather furniture and cream carpets was the first breath of urban living she'd gotten since she arrived here. While the Red Rock and Silver Springs packs leaned toward the rustic approach in their abodes, this place cost money. Navi wouldn't lie—it set off her internal alarms left and right.

"Want a cup of coffee?" Joe asked, heading into a kitchen that was all chrome backsplashes and porcelain tiled floors.

"How about a pot?" Finn asked, sauntering past her as he scanned the room. Even with the casual way he walked, his hands slipped into his pockets and shoulders back, the glow of vigilance hadn't faded from his eyes. She doubted the tension would leave him until Finn ripped out Dale Rossi's throat with his own fangs.

Their shaman friend set about to brewing a pot of coffee and, despite her concerns and the wary way she watched him pour out the roast, she could use a pick-me-up. She had gotten up far too early and the effects of her first two cups of java were wearing off.

"So, care to explain why I've got a member of the East Coast Tribe showing up on my doorstep this time of morning?" Joe asked, focusing on filling the coffeemaker with water. He pressed the button down and the machine let out a hiss, but he didn't look at her. No, not the slightest bit shady.

"Because Dale Rossi is distributing drugs in this territory courtesy of the Landsliders," Finn spoke up, leaving finesse and tact at the back door. Navi restrained her internal groan, rolling with the punches. Joe didn't look their way, didn't offer any surprise, and he also wasn't brimming with curiosity.

"I don't see how the drug runners of this region are any of my concern," Joe responded, leaning against his counter while the coffeemaker spat out tar-colored liquid, the robust scent curling through the room. His stance remained guarded, as it had been the moment they showed up. Not like his caution revealed any form of duplicity — anyone would be on edge with a random visit from the Tribe, and shamans doubly so.

Navi reached into her barely functional jeans pocket and tugged out a thumb-sized bag of white powder. "Because a shaman in this area happens to be working with them," she said, taking a cue from the Finn Kelly handbook and going straight for the kill. "I'd like to know if you're the one behind this magicked meth."

Joe still hadn't looked at her and Navi's claws pricked out at the ready, even though she kept her hands down.

"You'll have to bust down some other shaman's door," he said, remaining unruffled. "I stick to my own business out here." He poured three mugs of coffee before offering one to her and another to Finn. She sniffed the dark liquid on instinct, not trusting him in the slightest.

"I'll pay a visit to one of the shaman elders then," Navi said. Two could play at unruffled. Heading to the shaman elders would be inconvenient and take longer than she wanted, but he didn't need to know that. "They can trace whose magic is threaded through this meth and we can resolve this mystery quick and tidy-like." Navi watched, and waited. *Try to maneuver out of that, jackass.* Finn snorted at her side, a solid reminder to rope him in on a poker game so she could clean house.

Joe's grip tightened on his coffee mug until his knuckles were almost the same color as the porcelain. "I didn't have a choice," he murmured, meeting her gaze at last. Shame tugged at his frown, and his dark eyes burned with restrained anger. "It's not like we've got packs out here, or anyone else to protect us. My magic might be strong, but I'm not a match for an entire pack of shifters at my doorstep."

"Work with us and your situation will be taken into consideration," Navi commanded, her tone coming with the icy cool of her position. "Continue to protect Rossi and we'll haul you in now." Beside her, Finn tensed with readiness. Slight modifications to his stance—a pivot to his hip and a hunch forward. When she gave the signal, his wolf would be unleashed on this asshole before he could open his mouth to chant.

Navi clenched her jaw, sweeping away the thought he was her anything as her stomach twisted.

Joe heaved a sigh, and his shoulders sank with resignation. "What do you need from me?" he asked, his hands remaining wrapped around his mug. "I'm willing to help if you can ensure you'll take him out of the picture."

Finn clapped a hand on her shoulder and squeezed, drawing her attention his way. "Have you seen what this woman can do?" he asked. "The Tribe will make quick work of a lowlife like Ace." Navi didn't miss the way Joe's eyes narrowed in recognition at the name. Without a doubt, he had gotten deeply involved in this. Whether he told them the truth or not, if he could help them track Rossi, the other details didn't matter.

"We need to know where the main distribution is happening around here. We've already busted one of the trafficking spots, but if we don't take out Rossi and excise the Landsliders from the area, the problems will grow." Navi crossed her arms over her chest. "Don't suppose you performed the magic on location?"

Joe lifted his mug in salute. "Yeah, I worked with the big man himself. If locations are all you're looking for, they're yours. I don't want to keep living with the constant threat on my life if I don't cooperate. From either of you." He stalked over to his kitchen table where a silver laptop lay open. "What's your email?" he asked. Navi couldn't help but lift a brow in response. This urban, techie shaman was the furthest from the others of his kind she'd met.

Navi strolled over to his table, placing her mug on the lacquer surface. There was something she didn't like about Joe Ganzorig, but bias against shamans ran deep with her. They were the ones who'd imbued the spirit of the panther into her and marked her with these tattoos, the pain of the process forever engraved in her memory and on her body. She'd never quite been able to forgive them for stealing away her future. Navi typed her email into his computer, and he set to the keyboard, his fingers flying over the keys while he typed an address.

"So what exactly does this laced meth do?" she asked. "I'm not about to mess around with this shit to find out."

He shot a nervous glance her way. "A couple of different varieties are being produced. Some will amp up the animal side of you until you're berserker while others keep folks from shifting. I pretty much worked whatever spells they asked on the batches, no questions as to where they were being delivered or who was taking them."

"Fucking delightful," Navi muttered, running a hand through her hair. The last thing they needed to deal with on top of Mackey's compulsion tricks were 'roided out wolves and mountain lions. The Landsliders were a cancer determined to metastasize through this land.

Joe paused, glancing between them as his pointer finger hovered, ready to click Send. "If I do this, he's going to come for me. Meaning there's no margin for fucking up. I'm placing my life in your hands."

Navi bristled on instinct, annoyed at how the shaman acted like they wouldn't be able to handle this shifter and his crew, as though she hadn't handled thousands of these cases before. The acerbic words froze on her tongue when she caught the flash of fear in his eyes. The spirit of the panther chose her, not the shaman who performed the rite—they'd only been following through with what they'd agreed to do for the shifter community. Like always, the shamans were used and abused for their powers, more victims than anything. His fear made sense.

Before she could say anything, though, Finn stepped in. "I've got a personal grudge with Dale Rossi," he growled, the sound resonating through the small rancher. "He won't escape alive."

Joe's lips pressed tight together, but he nodded and hit Send. "I'm counting on the two of you, then."

Navi took an obligatory sip of coffee, which was still scorching, since this whole visit had gone much faster than anticipated. She placed the mug back on the countertop again. "Thanks for your help, Ganzorig. I know living around our kind can be dangerous for you guys."

Joe snorted, a bitter look crossing his face. "Humans, shifters, it doesn't matter. Our abilities are sought after to be used by just about everyone."

Navi nodded in response before she clapped a hand on Finn's shoulder. "Let's head out." Her chest squeezed tight. She understood the weight of being born into a power and position without being given a choice.

"Thanks, man," Finn called as they headed for the door. Navi slipped her phone out of her pocket, the cell vibrating in her hand when she received the email. They exited into the late-morning sunshine, the warmth not quite dispelling the discomfort from visiting Joe, or the unsettling tug inside that the whole encounter had been far too easy. Still, if they stealthed to scout the location, even if the Landsliders had set another trap, she'd know where to pin the blame. And if the entire East Coast Tribe bore down on Ganzorig, even a shaman like him wouldn't stand a chance.

Sweat pricked Navi's temple once they stepped into the humidity and she couldn't help how her heart sped on approach to her Plymouth. She glanced over at Finn. If they were doing any stealthing, it wouldn't be until after the sun set, but she wasn't ready to part ways with the Red Rock beta. Last night, she'd regretted the moment she left, frustration burning through her on multiple fronts. However, leaving had been the logical choice, necessary to keep her from leaping off the cliff into an unknown chasm.

"Does the Tribe pay you shit?" Finn asked, running a finger along the hood of her Plymouth. "I'd expect the lot of you to be driving around the country in style."

Navi snorted. "Yeah, my first foray with a sweet ride ended quick after the car got set on fire by a shifter convict we were chasing down. The next one got smashed to pieces when we were hunting a murderer in Massachusetts. After pouring so much time and work into them, I didn't have the heart to continue. I pretty much drive junkers at this point so my insurance company doesn't kill me." She hopped into the driver's seat and tapped the weathered wheel.

Finn shook his head as he settled into the passenger side. "I never considered that part of your job. You see action like this all the time?"

Navi started the ignition and pulled out of this lot, beginning the crawl through these narrow, unpaved roads. She had one destination in mind. "Every damn city. Folks don't call the Tribe in for tea. We're there to solve problems, protect the shifter citizens and apprehend the criminals in our sector."

"This summer's been the most action I've seen in a long time," Finn murmured, staring out of the window. "Sometimes it's hard not to feel like I'm wasting away."

Navi's heart pounded a few notches faster at the sincerity in his voice and how he opened up around her. She wished she could do the same, wished the words didn't stick in her throat every time she tried to speak about anything that squeezed her heart or flayed her insides. However, she wasn't made that way. She could bark orders until the end of time and keep level in the middle of an emergency, but truths remained her own, because they were the sole things she could cling onto with the constant change of her surroundings.

"Going to drop me off?" Finn asked, the seat creaking when he leaned back. She could feel his gaze burning into her, hotter than the blazing sun, hotter than the sticky humidity that descended today.

"I've got one stop to make first," she said, gripping the wheel tighter.

She wished for all the world she'd been born with a different purpose—as if the responsibility weighing down her life could melt away for one single moment. Like she could forget she was Tribe and simply be Navi Tremere.

Chapter Thirteen

Finn didn't want this car ride to end.

Every moment he spent with Navi, even while hunting the Landsliders, brought them closer together. He couldn't push himself to think about what would happen when she left, because after experiencing life with her in it, he didn't want to return to the hollowness without. Navi brimmed with nerves as she slammed on the gas, enough to make the car rattle. Finn wrestled with tension of his own, because he found it harder and harder to deny the desire warming his blood with every passing minute.

To top it off, he had no idea where she was taking him. Down this direction lay most of the Red Rock territory and they were about to pass his gym — which would be the perfect place to burn off all this unspent energy.

"You can drop me off at my gym," he said, the familiar turn in the highway coming up.

Navi cast him the side-eye. "Where did you think we were heading?"

Finn's brows came together in confusion. He didn't know why the woman remained close-lipped if she'd planned on dumping him off at his work, anyway. She still buzzed with tension, though, and he couldn't read her. Under the midday sun like this, that was where she glowed. The hint of gold in her tone came out in the rich brown and the thick, glossy strands of her pixie cut were illuminated. She looked like some sort of sun goddess and he wanted to lick every inch of her.

Kelly's Gym came into view and Navi slowed, pulling onto the beaten earth that constituted his parking lot. However, the lot wasn't empty. Parked right in front of the gym was a car he'd know anywhere—one he'd last seen bashed in at Jared's Auto.

"Figured you'd want to see your girl," Navi said when she put the Plymouth into Park. The hesitation in her voice sounded so different from the Tribe member who barked out orders and struck fear into the common shifter. These moments, the ones where she showed this secret side of herself, were worth fighting for.

He stepped out of the car before striding across the lot to his Challenger. After the way the bear had mauled the frame, the thing would need a lot of work done between replacing the tires, pounding out the dents, repainting and other detailing to buff out the scratches and blemishes that marred her. After all the time and elbow grease he'd put into his girl, watching the bear crush her in front of Jared's Auto had torn his heart out. Except as he stood before his Challenger, the dents and the scratches were all gone.

Footsteps sounded behind him as Navi approached. He could feel her presence, smell the vanilla and apple scent of her. "With the state she was in, the repairs were a challenge," she said, crossing her arms over her chest when she stopped beside him. "No pun intended. Never pun intended."

Finn reached out, running his hand along the smooth surface of his hood. While he knew his car well enough to notice the slight shifts in the paint where a fresh coat had been added on, the repair job was amazing. His throat tightened as overwhelming gratitude swept over him. Last night or this morning, she must have worked hours on this. He knew how much time it would have taken because he'd been trying to figure out when the hell he would be able to fix his girl.

She'd done all that — for him. Navi might not gush affection or talk emotion much, but this spoke volumes about the way she felt toward him. The woman had spent all this time and hard work fixing his car. Not out of duty, not out of any sense of guilt, but because she knew how much he loved this thing and she wanted to help. Fuck, if she wasn't everything he longed for, everything he hoped for, in a partner.

He wanted to kiss her, wanted to sweep her into his arms and make her scream his name. His feelings for Navi had become far too strong to be denied, but if he could take anything from this gesture, words weren't her forte. Fine then. He'd take a page from her book of actions. The way she glanced to him, the shyness in her glance was so opposite to the sensual, confident woman he'd first met, but the more he'd gotten to know her, the more he understood the vulnerable girl who resided within the fierce Tribe member, one who'd never gotten a childhood.

His palm grew warm from resting it on the hood of his fixed-up Challenger, and the warmth traveled straight to his chest. Finn turned to face Navi, only separated from her by agonizing inches. Desire gleamed in her eyes as she met his gaze, the sort that brought him to his knees. She pursed her full lips together as if she mused on something, but she was always thinking, always worrying. He wanted to take away those worries until she existed in the moment.

He knew why they'd broken off their kiss the other night and why she'd left the party. Because what had developed between them ran much deeper than a one-night stand. The intensity of his feelings for Navi Tremere held the promise to mark him forever. However, even if she left him in the dust, even if this all crashed and burned, he'd forever regret not taking the time while he had the chance.

Finn stepped forward, crossing the space between them. He slipped his hand against her cheek and dipped to press his mouth to hers.

The moment they kissed, everything else melted away. The trucks rumbling along the highway, the birds chirping in the trees — everything grew distant compared to the honeyed taste of her. His lips caressed hers, coaxing her mouth open until he slipped his tongue inside. She twined her arms around him, her nails digging into his back in a possessive way that traveled straight to his cock. He wrapped his hands around her waist, those powerful curves sharpening his desire.

Finn leaned her against the car, needing to feel the heat of her against his skin. She moaned against his mouth as they pressed together, his cock stiffening in his jeans. This wasn't enough — would never be enough for him. He wanted to taste her, to show gratitude for how she reached him. For the depth of emotion she stirred inside him. Finn grabbed her by the hips until he slid his hands around her ass to lift her against him. She wrapped her thighs around his hips and a low groan slipped from him. The urge to drive into her mounted in both man and wolf until he could barely register more than the deafening roar of his desire.

Finn pulled away from her mouth to look at Navi, her full lips swollen and a dusky flush on her cheeks. "Do or die time, babe," he murmured against her mouth. "You let this beast off the leash and I'm not going to stop."

Her mouth curled into a sensual smile, and her hazel eyes glowed with the challenge. "Do your worst, Finn Kelly."

His name on her lips was like a caress and he couldn't help how his heart pounded double time. Those words ratcheted his need, driving him to deliriousness. With a few powerful strides, he carried her over to the hood of his Challenger and he lowered her there. Navi propped herself up by the elbows, her brow lifted.

"Here?" she asked. "There's a highway, right there."

His lips curled into a smile and his gaze heated with the heady dose of lust rushing through him. "Panties off, now," he growled.

Her lips pursed and, for a moment, he thought the mighty Tribe member would object at taking the order from him. But she'd been giving orders her entire life, and here and now, he wanted to take the burden from her.

She unsnapped the button of her jean shorts, the snick echoing in the air. He didn't hesitate, tearing them off her the rest of the way, panties to the ground too. The sun glowed on her ebony skin, bringing out the golden hues, the vanilla scent of her making him want to sink his teeth in. Her Tribe tattoos traveled her muscular legs, drawing his attention up and up.

"Spread your legs," he ordered, the need to taste her driving him in a fierce way. She complied, desire burning in her eyes. "Good girl," he murmured, before leaning over the car and situating himself between her legs. Her dark curls were damp and her pussy glistened. God, she was positively fuckable.

He dipped down to take the first taste. The moment he glided his tongue over her clit, she let out a low noise deep in her throat that made his balls ache. He continued to lap at her hot pussy, quickening the rhythm of his tongue to her clit. With each stroke, she bucked forward, responsive, and sexily draped against the hood of his Challenger. Her thighs tightened around his head as he increased his crescendo, and he pulled away for a moment to sink his teeth into the sensitive skin of her inner thigh.

Her back arched at the contact as she thrust her pussy forward for him. He dipped down again, slipping his tongue past her folds and driving it into her center. Her loud cry pierced the air and he continued to fuck her with his mouth, adoring the way she cried out for him, damn the fact that they were out here under the broad sunlight, in front of the highway. The whole experience dizzied him with lust, indulging in fantasies too hot to have imagined.

Finn bit her thigh again, enjoying the way she writhed beneath him while he slipped his fingers into her hot folds. She clenched around his fingers at the contact, and he slid them in and out, faster and faster. Her breathing quickened and sweat beaded her soft-as-silk skin. She bucked beneath him, her palms flat against the hood of his car as her back curved in response to the increased pressure when he finger-fucked her. She was the sort of woman unashamed of her sexuality, bold and brazen as a dream, but watching her moan his name was unforgettable.

Her cries reached a fever pitch and her thighs tightened while he continued to kiss and suck her skin until her legs began to tremble. She arched again, holding it this time as her core clenched around his fingers, the spasms radiating in the aftermath. Slowly, Finn pulled his fingers from her dripping pussy and he prowled up the length of her body to claim her lips. Her kisses in return were slow, sensual and sated.

The pulse of his erection reached a painful point and he couldn't deny the intense need mounting in him. Navi nipped and sucked at the skin on his neck, the sensation traveling straight south.

"God, I want to be inside you," he murmured into her ear. She shivered beneath him and he tightened his grip around her hips as he leaned down to suck her earlobe. The following moan made it harder to think straight.

Navi slid off the top of the car, her gaze dusky when she looked at him, tilting her head toward the gym. "Come on then," she said, the sensuality in her voice a caress. "Let's get sweaty on the mats."

Chapter Fourteen

Navi didn't think she'd ever been so turned on when Finn devoured her on top of his Challenger. Yet, even after one of the most intense orgasms of her life, her core sparked to awareness again the second she heard the snick of the gym door shut behind her, knowing what would be coming next. Each step farther inside surrounded her with the scent of sweat, leather and wood polish—the scent of him. Her panther preened inside her chest with a newfound restlessness to seal the deal.

Her bare pussy dripped and she clenched her thighs together as a light shiver traveled through her in anticipation. He approached behind her, his shadow looming and his presence radiating such an intense warmth that even this August heat couldn't compete. The logical part of her raged inside her chest at crossing this line and allowing herself to head down this path again when it would end in hurt and pain. But Navi wanted him with a strength and fury she'd never experienced before, so the logical part of herself could fuck off.

She was tired of running and tired of denying herself out of fear. She'd deal with the crash and burn when she left, but, here and now, she wanted Finn Kelly.

Navi turned around to face Finn, who stood inches away from her. The space between them charged like an electricity storm, filled with all the things they couldn't say. Even though her limbs were loose from the way he'd pounced on her outside, her core thrummed with anticipation, with the aching need to be filled. She wanted to take every formidable inch of him inside her.

She reached out, trailing one finger down his shirt, the flimsy fabric sticking to his chest with sweat. "Let's even the playing field a little," she murmured. "This, off."

He complied with a delicious smirk on his lips that she wanted to sink her teeth into. The fabric dropped to the ground and he moved his hand to the button of his pants.

Navi placed her hand over his, stopping him. "Let me," she said, wildness surging under the surface, her panther present in every step of this. The first time they'd clashed together had been hot, passionate and unforgettable, but here and now, she knew this moment would be with her until she expired. She undid the button and slipped the zipper down, trailing her tongue over her lips in anticipation.

Finn didn't waste time, shucking his pants down before tugging at her shirt. "This comes off too," he said, slipping his hands underneath the fabric to snap the back of her bra. She yanked her shirt off and tossed it to the mats, her bra following. Her nipples tightened the minute they were exposed to the air. Finn reached forward to cup her breasts and glided his thumbs over the tips. She bit her lip to keep from crying out at the sensation flooding through her, at how responsive her body was to his touch.

"You're fucking gorgeous," he breathed, his gaze darkening with desire. He stood inches away from her, his erection stark between them, causing her core to throb in needy anticipation.

"And you're mine, Finn Kelly." The words came from her before she could help herself, an admission she'd never allowed before. The response descended like a storm. Finn's eyes glowed, the wolf as present as her panther, the connection between them deeper than just physical. He wrapped his hands around her thighs, hoisting her up and around him. Her breasts pressed against his bare chest, and the brush of her nipples across those hard planes sent her senses into overdrive until she grew drenched.

He strode with her in his arms the couple of paces until her back slammed against the wall. Finn brimmed with aggression in the best way, the fearlessness that drew her to him in the first place. She leaned in, pressing her lips to his throat. He lifted his chin to bare his throat, and she lightly scraped her teeth against the exposed skin. A low growl escaped him in the process and a moment later she could feel the hot steel of his cock against her thigh. She was soaked, dripping wet for him, and the tightness increased with every stroke, every bite and every touch.

"I need you inside me," she gasped out, driven half to madness with the friction of her nipples against his chest and the heat of his erection rubbing against her inner thigh. If he didn't take her now, she was liable to explode.

Finn hoisted her up, digging his fingers into her hips. Without preamble, he thrust straight into her.

Navi's thighs tightened, her core clenched, and bliss rocked through her from his thickness and the way he filled her to completion. She tilted her hips toward him, grinding her heels into his ass as he pulled back, only to drive into her again and again. Her sensitized clit caused her to gasp every time they clashed together, and the scent of him, all leather and sweat, created a heady swirl with each breath.

Their lips met in a ferocious frenzy of teeth and tongues while he rammed into her with building intensity. He lifted her as though she weighed nothing, and as her back slammed against the wall with the passion of his thrusts, she'd never felt so claimed. Hell, she'd never trusted anyone like she trusted him in both body and mind. The pulse inside her core built, increasing every time he sank into her.

He nipped at the sensitive skin between her neck and her shoulder, hard enough to send a dizzying rush through her. Navi sank her nails into his back as she clutched him, surrendering to the pleasure that threatened to carry her away. Drops of sweat rolled down her back and she shuddered at the bliss rolling through her with every movement. Each time he thrust into her, the delicious smack of her clit against him, the blaze of desire in his deep brown eyes and his enduring strength and steadiness pushed her closer and closer to the ledge.

Her core tightened, to the point that her mind blanked and a scream ripped from her throat. Sweat beaded her forehead when she came, her pussy pulsing with her orgasm. Heat poured into her as he dug his nails into her hips. His cock kicked inside her with his release, while he emptied into her.

As she rode the waves of her orgasm, a feeling of rightness settled in her, so strong she almost lost her grip on Finn. He sagged against her, crushing her against the wall. He pressed his mouth to hers in a kiss utterly gentle compared to the wild way they'd bucked together seconds before. In the moment, she felt like a knot had been tied, an inviolable tether to him. Her panther stopped still, a predator's awareness that brought her out of the hazy bliss of her release.

Finn's eyes blinked open, the wolf glowing in them for a brief moment. "Did you feel that?" he asked, his voice low and husky. Slowly, he sank to the ground with her, his grip never wavering. Her feet settled onto the mats, but she couldn't help the breathlessness overtaking her or the way she floated.

Mine.

The word gripped her by the throat when the realization descended. Finn bared his teeth, fangs coming out in response to the surge between them.

"Oh fuck," she murmured before she could help herself. She sank forward, burying her head in his chest. This wasn't supposed to happen. Not to her. Navi was Tribe. She was the one forever tethered to the road, to whatever job required their supervision and help. Tribe traveled a wild and dangerous path not meant for attachments, but this—this was the most permanent sort of attachment among shifter kind.

"Was that the mating bond?" Finn asked. He tipped her chin up with his finger, searching her face as if she held all the answers.

A hysterical laugh slipped from her throat before she could help herself. Unadulterated joy was supposed to come with this connection, but the first buzzing of anxiety rushed through her in one suffocating sweep. *No, no, no.* Finn wasn't meant for a life on the road like she lived. He had a place here — a family, a home and a role in his community. If she tore him from that, she'd ruin him, but now that they'd mated, they would live half-lives apart.

Finn drew his brows together, a frown on his face. His thumb smoothed creases along her forehead she didn't realize were there. "What's wrong?" he asked.

"I…" She trailed off as the hysteria tightened her throat, the buzzing threatening to overwhelm her. Too much, too fast. "I'm Tribe." She forced the words out. "We're not meant for mates."

"Well, I think the fates are determined to prove otherwise," he responded, his voice soft and gentler than she could imagine from the man who radiated fire and passion. He swallowed, glancing away for a moment. "I know we didn't get a chance to talk things over, but is it really so terrible?" he asked. "Being mated to me?"

Her grip on him tightened, the vulnerability in his words hanging suspended in the air between them. She could taste his pain, feel those pangs like they were her own with the completeness of their connection.

Navi's chest ached with confusion. She wanted him to desperation, the silent thrill coursing through her veins at the idea of that impenetrable connection. However, the choking, earth-shattering fear followed, that she was given a taste of this only to have it stolen away. Just like her hopes had been crushed in every other town and every other job.

"I've never met anyone I wanted the way I want you, Finn," Navi whispered, her skin prickling at opening up to him like this. They sat crouched in front of each other, both buck naked, yet this exposed her far more. "But I can't ignore who I am. This is the duty that was branded on me here," she said, lifting up her arms, the tattoos so, so clear. "You deserve the chance at a real life with your family and friends. I couldn't take you away from that." The admission tore her to shreds and the panther inside growled at the idea of separation.

Finn tilted her chin again and brushed his lips to hers. She sank into the taste of him and reveled at how his scent imprinted on her memory, deeper than skin. For a single moment, the panic and the fear subsided, and she surrendered to the calm of his kiss, his touch a lifeline.

He broke away from her lips but wrapped his arms around to pull her in tight. "I've never met anyone who completes me the way you do, Navi Tremere," he said. With her head to his chest, his words rumbled. "Neither of us planned to find our mate, but now that I have you in my life, you've got to be crazy to think I'd let you go."

The heat in his voice and the tender way he held her — too much. It cracked her wide open, the arctic, remote part of herself she shut off from ever considering anything like this. The little girl who'd lost the ability to hope long ago.

Navi swallowed, her throat tightening on instinct. His strength seeped through to her, and not just from the honed muscles of a tested warrior, but at how he indulged his emotions in a way she'd never permitted herself to. Warmth saturated her chest, the sort of cinnamon scorch that left marks.

Finn Kelly was her mate.

The revelation surged through her with the strength to make her ache, even as she fought with the corners of her mouth threatening to break into a smile. Giddiness whirled through her like the first sunlit day of spring. She hadn't dared to hope a mate waited for her out there. Navi had convinced herself she would walk a lonely path until the day she died.

Except here he crouched before her, all breakable brown eyes, old scars and the shortest temper she'd ever encountered. And unlike every other guy she'd messed around with before, this was the one man she couldn't shake.

Once a real smile emerged on her face, she was screwed. As fast as the elation rushed through her, the fear flowed so much faster. Her brief gasp of joy got smothered by the deadening hopelessness that infiltrated over too many years of disappointments and missed connections. Navi had given up trying to find someone, because she knew their story would end. She knew she would have to leave.

And she understood with a keen clarity that if she had to leave Finn now, after knowing what existed between them and indulging in the radiant warmth and comfort of finding her mate, she would be destroyed. No one on this earth could put those pieces together again.

"I thought you knew off the bat when you found your mate," Finn murmured into her hair. "How come we didn't get any heads-up the first time we fucked?"

Navi sucked in a sharp breath, grabbing onto the distraction like a lifeline. Facts and information — that was safe territory. She pulled away from his embrace to sit on one of the mats, splaying her legs out in front of her. While she had no qualms with nudity — few shifters did—she also didn't make a habit of sitting around naked with anyone, not after the sort of fireworks that had exploded between them. However, Finn was different. She'd been meant for him all along.

"Because the mating bond is as simple and complicated as we are," she responded. As one of the Tribe who oversaw the mating ceremonies, she'd learned far too much over the years about something she believed impossible for herself. Something she yearned for to the secret depths of her soul.

"Dax and Sierra happened to find their connection the moment they met each other," she continued, leaning back on her palms.

"Isn't that normal?" Finn's gaze traveled her body, the heat still visible there.

Navi resisted the flare of satisfaction at how he blazed for her even after sated. If she could hold on to this, for even a moment, maybe she'd have something to remember on lonely nights to come. Her throat tightened while she struggled to breathe. *Focus.*

"Both were in heightened situations where their emotions were on display whether they liked it or not." Navi forced herself to keep talking, if only to quiet her mind. "Others have been around their mates for years without realizing, sometimes because the partners aren't yet who they're meant to be. In our case, you were too involved with Raven and I was too shielded for the bond to ever manifest loud enough to notice."

"You sure it wasn't the sheer amount I rocked your world?" Finn responded with a wink. He prowled toward her until he crouched in front of her, his presence igniting her body like a livewire.

Navi shot him a look. "I'm apparently mated to an idiot. You'd think for one of the Great Spirits, my panther would have better selective skills."

He leaned in to steal another kiss and Navi indulged him, unable to deny the honeyed bliss of his mouth. When she pulled away, the boyish grin on his lips and the twinkle in his eyes made her heart race. Finn basked in their discovery in a way she never could. He'd dealt with his own damage in the past, but he knew how to connect with others with experience but also an innate naturalness. Whereas Navi—she tended to stick to business, and even with her closest, those guards always remained up.

In the brief time she'd spent among the Red Rock pack, Finn Kelly had brought those guards tumbling down. He'd rammed at them and clawed until he'd coaxed her out from hiding. Until they'd bonded in a way she could no longer deny, in a way that would mark her for the rest of her days.

There were a thousand different worries running through her mind and a thousand different ways the timeworn fear tried to infiltrate, but here in his presence, she took a leaf from Finn's book. Right now, she could focus on the present. They had a Landslider drug-running operation to scout and a certain Dale Rossi to confront.

Fighting was familiar territory—those risks, they were ones she could handle. Pain, adrenaline, physical aggression were all in her wheelhouse. None of those froze her like the intensity of everything that threatened to rush through her every time Finn looked at her with those eyes promising the forever she'd never get.

"Sun hasn't set yet," she said, pulling away from him to reclaim her strewn-about clothes. "Let's grab a pint before we scout the warehouse."

Chapter Fifteen

Settled into the driver's seat of his Challenger with his mate by his side, Finn couldn't have been more elated. Sure, he'd have some tough decisions to figure out in the future, but he knew he didn't want to let her go. Fuck, he couldn't have imagined he'd ever find someone as perfect as Navi Tremere.

He tightened his grip on the steering wheel while he raced down the highway in the direction of Beaver Tavern, the path he'd traveled a thousand times. Except this time he wouldn't be entering the bar to chat up Raven for some action or hunker down with Sierra to discuss pack business. This time he was grabbing a pint with his mate. Who brimmed with enough tension to ignite the air.

The familiar building rose in the distance on his right, the cream exterior glowing under the sun, and the dark wooden accents adding to the cozy feel. Already a couple of cars clustered in the gravel parking lot, since the bar would soon be in full swing once the sun set.

Finn wheeled his car down the ramp before pulling into a spot. Navi glanced at him, caution glowing in her hazel eyes. She'd lapsed into a tense silence ever since they'd realized they had mated.

Finn reached over and placed his hand on her thigh, the thrill of touching her this freely one he hoped he never lost. "I know I'm a hot commodity, but you're not going to have to battle the entire pack for me," he said, flashing her a grin.

Navi gave him a flat look, amusing him further. Even with the 'no bullshit' expression she delivered, her hand rested over his and she squeezed. "We haven't even discussed what we're going to do. They don't need to get into our business. Not yet."

Finn snorted and with reluctance pulled his hand away as he reached for the door handle. "Babe, you must've met the wrong pack. Everyone is in each other's business morning, noon and night."

"Joy," she muttered, hopping out of the car. Finn approached beside her, skimming his fingers across her shoulders. She jumped at his touch, wheeling around with her shoulders braced to attack.

"We don't have to go here if you don't want to," he said, realizing how on edge she was.

Navi let out a sigh. "What, and go to the one other diner you've got in this neck of the woods? We're not spoiled for choices here." She strode toward the bar. "Come on, let's get some grub. If I don't carb up soon, I'm liable to Hulk out."

He quickened his pace, his long legs helping him reach the door before her. Finn grabbed the handle, unable to shake the giddiness clinging to him, the feeling of rightness that gripped him around her. This was what he'd been searching for all these years, the reason he'd never made Raven any promises. Deep in his gut, both he and his wolf knew Navi was meant for him, that she was the one he wanted to spend the rest of his days with. He'd had an inkling when she had first walked into this bar with the rest of the Tribe, but every moment they'd spent together had caused that feeling to grow until it roared in his mind with the ferocity of a hurricane that drowned out any doubts.

As they stepped into Beaver Tavern, the familiar scents of porter and wood polish wafted his way and, already, Jer stood around one of the pool tables, cue poised at the ready. Sierra sat at the bar, a stack of papers in front of her, which meant she'd already descended into business mode. Meanwhile, Kyle, one of the mountain lions from the Silver Springs pack, roamed behind the bar, the new bartender to replace Seamus.

After Jer had made his next move, he leaned the pool cue against the green felt table and approached. Finn could feel the tension radiating off Navi as thick in the air as the summer heat. As much as he wanted to shout their news to the rooftops, he wasn't going to put her through the scrutiny right now.

Their pack lawyer scrunched his features while he scanned them over. "What's going on?" Jer asked, the man too perceptive for his own good. "Something changed between you guys."

Navi shook her head, but instead of responding she strode straight to the bar. Finn clapped a hand on Jer's shoulder, avoiding his eyes even though he couldn't restrain his smile. "Nothing happened," he said, attempting to avoid the news like Navi wished.

Jer lifted his brow. "Bullshit, brother. You're the worst liar in the region."

Finn ran a hand over his buzz cut, unable to backtrack around that one as he headed toward the bar. "Come on, let's get ourselves a drink."

Jer remained quiet, the shrewdness in his eyes something not everyone understood about him on first glance. Most women and, hell, some guys were too distracted by the winsome smiles, the tousled chestnut hair and the flirty comments. Finn knew his best friend better. Sierra pivoted in her seat to face them upon approach, and Navi claimed the stool beside her with two pints in hand.

"You're a goddess," Finn said, accepting the pint from his mate. She ducked her head for a moment in embarrassment, the motion so adorable he gave up restraining his giddy grin. Sierra hadn't said a word yet, watching both of them like they'd started a sparring match. Finn lifted the pint of Guinness to his lips, trying to ignore the way his packmates were analyzing him.

"I ordered burgers," Navi said, locking gazes with him while she moved uncomfortably in her stool. "If that's not what you wanted, tough. I'll eat both of them." She radiated the guarded Tribe member he first met, all official business with a rough edge he had believed was impenetrable. Finn couldn't be happier at how she'd proved him wrong.

"They're ordering food together." Jer leaned in to Sierra as he delivered a stage whisper. "What do you think of that?"

Finn shot his best friend a glare. Asshole would milk this drama until he pulled the answers out of him.

"I think Finn bit off more than he can chew," Sierra responded, giving Navi a wink. Navi tried to force a smile in return even though she lifted her gaze to shoot him a look. She was right. The moment they spilled their news, this would get complicated and fast. Finn tipped back his pint, the realization settling in at last how complicated this could become. Navi would never be able to stay here—she was Tribe, and her calling took priority over his role as pack beta every time.

Could he even live like that? On the road all the time, thrust into danger and never having the camaraderie and closeness he did here? The first pinpricks of nerves traveled along his arms. He had left the pack once when his folks had dragged him away, and they'd hopped from motel to motel all over this region. He'd hated every second of it.

No matter the encroaching doubts, no matter the worries that buzzed in the back of his head, nothing could conquer the sense of fulfillment, the rightness that marked him once their bond solidified. Sure, they had a long and twisted road ahead of them, but the sight of Navi, her presence alone quelled the restlessness of his wolf that had plagued him for a long time now.

"You can do better than this guy," Jer said, slinking beside Navi with a charmer twinkle in his eye. Streaky had earned his reputation with the ladies because he literally couldn't keep off them. His grip tightened on his pint glass while Jer stood within an inch of her, throwing all his ladykiller charm her way. Navi didn't bat an eye, watching him with a wan look and a light, almost lethal smile on her face.

Sierra's gaze sharpened. She stared at him like he'd caught on fire. "Finn, you're growling."

He blinked and closed his mouth, the rumble in his chest dying down. He hadn't even realized he'd started. Finn tilted back his porter and chugged in an attempt to distract, but too late. Sierra watched him with interest and now Jer's attention swung their way. His alpha hadn't won her position through brawn, though—the woman was sharp as a tack. And with her glances alternating between Finn and Navi, he couldn't help the sinking feeling she knew.

"You're mated." Sierra's response rang through the loaded quiet, no hesitation in her voice. When he didn't respond at once, he'd already sentenced himself. Jer's jaw dropped and, at once, he backed away from Navi as if she'd burst on fire.

Finn worked his jaw for a few moments, not sure what the hell to say. The quiet that descended wasn't the exultation he'd hoped for. Congratulations weren't flying from their lips, so they must've leapt straight to the potential ramifications portion of the news.

Navi let out a low sigh and placed her pint on the smooth chestnut surface of the bar. "Look, before you lot go jumping to conclusions, we just came to this realization." She fixed her gaze on Sierra. "You, of all people, should understand how confusing that can be. We haven't discussed shit about the future, so if you've got questions, keep them to yourselves." Her tone didn't falter from the brisk no-nonsense she doled out to most folks. No one but a Tribe member would have the brass balls to talk to Sierra that way, not with the ferocious reputation the Red Rock alpha maintained.

Jer shook his head as if he was clearing the clouds from his brain and he extended his hand in Finn's direction. Finn clapped his palm over his best friend's and the man brought him in for a hug.

"I'm damn happy for you," Jer said. His fierce embrace flooded Finn with the sort of warmth he'd never be able to shake, the reminder of where his home was—where he belonged. As much as he and Jer had butted heads over the years, he would never find a better friend. The man had stood by him throughout the Raven drama and through picking fights in shifter and human bars alike back when the old alpha was still alive. Hell, Jer was one of the first friends he'd made upon returning to the pack after his parents passed away.

As Jer stepped back, Sierra clapped a hand on his shoulder. "Knew it would happen someday, Kelly. Good for you." Despite the level tone in her voice, he'd known his alpha long enough to read the turbulence in her eyes. Knowing Sierra, she was thinking of the future like Navi had. Of the potential problems to arise if he chose to leave.

Finn couldn't help the irritation burning in his chest. When she and Dax had discovered they were mates, he'd been her support through all the ups and downs, despite the changes that traveled down the pipeline— despite the way his position as her right-hand man had become defunct. Still, he'd never said a word.

"Because that sounded real genuine, Kanoska." The words came from his mouth before he could help himself. Her eyes narrowed in response. "Would it kill you to be a friend for once rather than an alpha? I think I've earned that."

"Screw you," she responded, the level tone discarded in the flare of temper his alpha wielded. "My duty isn't something I can pick up and take off as I choose. You'd think, of all people, you'd get that, beta."

Finn's nails transformed into claws, his temper rising to a fever pitch. He needed to get the hell out of there before he slammed his fist through the newly fixed walls. "Get fucked. Do you think I'm going to be satisfied wasting away here as your second-in-command the rest of my life?" His words came out in a growl and he couldn't help the flames burning his chest, scorching his mind, and driving the words that descended like bombs.

Sierra's gaze darkened, the glitter in her eyes dangerous.

"Kyle, get the burgers to go," Navi called over to the bartender. The mountain lion shifter near bolted to the back when he caught sight of the situation brewing out front. Finn bared his fangs, not bothering to hide the rage that tore through him. Everything he'd kept to himself all this time, every small sacrifice and every burden he bore on his lonesome came rushing to the surface here and now.

Sierra stood from her seat with the screech of the legs against the hardwood as she faced him. He placed his pint down in the process. If she wanted a go at him, he'd be happy to oblige. Jer watched, mouth sealed shut.

"You're big on the talk, Finn. Let's see if you've gotten any better from the last time we fought," she responded, her words dripping with condescension. She tried to rile him up and the attempt worked. The scar on his brow throbbed on instinct from the phantom memories of how she'd sliced into it during their alpha fight. Back then, he'd convinced himself he was fine with coming in second. Yet ever since then, his wolf had grown more and more agitated with the passing years, something he hadn't shared with a soul.

Kyle raced up with a plastic to-go bag and passed it across the bar to Navi.

"As much as I'd pay good money to watch a fight between the two of you, we have a warehouse to scout," Navi drawled, her cool voice slicing through the tension weighing down the air. "I can't have you injured and not at top efficiency against the Landsliders because you got into a scrap here." The brazen woman grabbed the bag off the counter and stepped square between them, facing Sierra.

His alpha bared her teeth at Navi and he couldn't help the growl surging from his throat.

"Don't worry, Finn," Navi called to him. "If she doesn't comply, she can try her luck against me. I guarantee the fight won't last more than a second. And if you're worried about her getting hurt, I'll compel her to back down."

Sierra's gaze glittered with rage, but she stepped away. His alpha might have a temper, but she would always act in the best interest of the pack. And royally pissing off one of the East Coast Tribe wasn't in the best interest of the Red Rocks.

"Take him," Sierra shot back, glancing at him. "He doesn't want to be here, anyway."

Her words stung, but Navi's level voice broke through the haze of his rage. He nodded a goodbye to Jer, ignored Sierra and took off at a clipped pace after Navi as she made her way to the door. Stares burned through him while he passed by packmates he'd grown up with. Yet if the pack had to choose between him or Sierra, he knew who they'd side with every time. He quickened his steps until he burst outside of the bar.

Orange and gold streaks overtook the sky, some fuchsia mingling throughout as the sun made its descent. He couldn't help but find it fitting that he was watching this sunset from Beaver Tavern, watching the dissolution of a day that had been filled with revelations and upheavals, ones that promised to disrupt the course of his life for good. Finn ran a hand through the short fuzz of his buzz cut, unable to focus with the anger that throbbed through him.

He strode over to his Challenger and found a spot to lean while he fought the rage making his hands tremble. Inside, Sierra had to be equally pissed. Navi perched against the side and opened the to-go bag. She passed him a Styrofoam container with the scents of salty cheddar and rich beef. His stomach rumbled, but until he flipped the lid open to the freshly grilled bacon cheeseburger and fries, he didn't realize how hungry he was. Navi began tucking into hers, grace forgotten in the haste to get food into her mouth.

He dove in with equal abandon, the tang of cheese and bacon exploding on his tongue and the juices dripping from the perfectly cooked beef. Finn polished the burger off in a few bites and did a number on the fries, licking the salt from his fingers afterward. The two of them leaned on his car, shoveling the contents of the containers into their mouths with barely a word in edgewise. As he popped the last couple of fries into his mouth, he blinked, realizing the haze of rage had settled. The incident drove a sharp knife to the gut still, but he could at least think clearly.

Navi pointed with a fry back in the direction of Beaver Tavern. "Not like I wasn't willing to watch you go toe-to-toe with her for the sake of a good fight, but the two of you were about to say and do things you'd both regret."

Finn let out a sigh, slumping against his Challenger as he plunked his hands into his pockets. "Yeah. Fuck, that could've gone better," he said, staring at the gravel driveway at his feet. Out of everyone, he'd thought Sierra would get how the mating bond could come in and upheave your life. She'd pretty much merged the packs when she found her mate, and he'd gone along without complaint. Yet when even the hint of a shake-up to her world hit, she couldn't put on her big girl pants to be happy for him.

"She's just upset, you know," Navi murmured, her voice low. "You're a family here, and she can't come to grips with the idea you might not be around. I might not know Sierra well, but I can say, if she didn't respect the absolute hell out of you, she wouldn't have had you by her side at the mating ceremony. The woman might duck behind her role as alpha, but anyone can see she sure as hell isn't ready to let you go."

Finn's chest squeezed tight. Navi was dead on the mark and he knew it. He'd let his own damage blind him to something he should've known from the get-go. His alpha hated change with a ferocity, and if he chose to go with the Tribe — hell, if Navi would even have him on the road with her — this would be a big one.

"That'll pale in comparison to the conversation I need to have with Raven." He scrubbed his face, not wanting to even think of the nightmare. She'd been so unwilling to accept him moving on, but the fact that he'd found his mate had the potential to shatter her. As much as she might delude herself, this evidence wasn't the sort she could strike up an argument against.

Navi let out a sharp growl at the mention of Raven, her eyes glowing silver with her panther. He couldn't help the thrum of amusement at the jealousy from his mate. He leaned in to brush his mouth against hers, tasting the salt from the fries.

"You're mine," he murmured. "The talk with Raven was a long time coming, but there is no hesitation in my mind when it comes to you. I waited ages for this — to feel so complete."

She wrapped her arms around him, kissing him in return, a soft, sensual sweep of her lips. The tenderness in the gesture communicated everything the woman might not be willing to say. Everything she couldn't admit.

Navi pulled back even though her arms still wrapped around him, and she fixed him with an arch look. "Enough of the sweet talking, Romeo," she said. "We've got a warehouse to scout."

Finn cast a glance to Beaver Tavern. He didn't like leaving things this way between him and Sierra, but while their tempers blazed, nothing good would be accomplished. He only hoped the rift between them wasn't permanent.

Chapter Sixteen

As much as she'd hoped to keep their mating a secret, the moment Navi had spotted Sierra and Jer in Beaver Tavern, her plan had gone up in flames. Finn couldn't hide his emotions when he tried, and most of the time he was too blunt and forward to even attempt subtlety. Navi couldn't deny that was one of the things she liked about him most.

She ran a hand over the askew pieces of her pixie cut, trying to ignore the sticky sweat clinging to her even with the cool breezes the descending night brought. Navi and Finn flew across the highway, Finn gunning the gas pedal to release some pent-up aggression after the way he and his alpha had butted heads back there.

Navi cast a glance his way, unable to reconcile the idea that this gorgeous, ferocious man was hers. Night stretched long shadows over his face, bringing out the arch of his nose, the stubborn jaw, and deepening the scar along his eyebrow as well as the ones littering his neck and arms from countless years of fighting. Despite all his taut muscle and the scowl twisting his features, his dark eyes held a softness betraying the truth of the man inside. He had a big heart, bigger than most — beyond that, a vulnerability from his past scars and mistakes that made her chest ache.

In the distance, the soft glow of a floodlight illuminated a plot of warehouses, the aluminum siding reflecting against the beams. On the plus, at least their friendly local shaman had given them the right site, since these were the exact sort of warehouses they'd been searching for. Now they just needed to figure out if he'd tipped off Rossi or not. If they stumbled into an emptied and cleared-out warehouse or, worse, one with a crew of Landsliders hiding in wait, Navi would be paying Joe another surprise visit and that one wouldn't be a casual chat over coffee.

Finn pulled to the side of the road, finding a patch of unpaved dirt before the clearing opened up to the warehouses. Tall grasses and bushes obscured his Challenger from view.

"Are you going to be okay with seeing Rossi again?" Navi asked when the car settled into Park and he shut off the engine.

Finn shrugged. "I'll have to be. I won't let my temper compromise our position." Even with the casual way he spoke, Finn brimmed with an unspoken tension and his mouth formed a hard line. Navi reached over to squeeze his hand, half in disbelief at the connection that had formed between them. Never in her life had she been able to touch someone so effortlessly without complicated signals or the wall that existed between her and near everyone else on this planet.

He grinned, returning the squeeze. "You're one in a million, Tremere. Let's go track this bastard down."

She nodded, hopping out of the passenger side. Navi glanced at the road, but no cars approached in the distance. She crouched out of view on her side of the Challenger and Finn joined her as they stripped, crumpling clothing into balls before tossing them back inside the car. If stealth was required, only one form would do. Even as she straightened to begin her shift, she couldn't help admiring the view of the man who'd been inside her hours earlier or dismiss the memories of how he'd wrung her dry of every last orgasm.

Focus. Navi forced her gaze to the car in front of her as she let the panther free. Fur sprouted along her arms and legs and her bones began to shift with the transition onto all fours. In this form, the night grew brighter, the crisp metallic scents sharper and the trills of cicadas more resonant. She arched her back in her panther form, her claws digging into the ground with her stretch. Finn's wolf was a beautiful russet color, and he padded toward her to brush his muzzle against hers. Her panther preened at the constant affection. Navi had cut herself off from that nonsense until the animal side of her had grown touch-starved. However, Finn just might shower her in enough affection to make up for all those years.

Navi headbutted him lightly before trekking past Finn in the direction of the warehouses. With her heightened senses, she could hear the rustle of movement from inside and the gentle murmur of voices, meaning they weren't heading into a cleared-out place. However, that also meant, if they got caught, they'd be facing whatever shifters or humans Rossi employed.

She padded toward the warehouse with the silent stealth afforded to her kind, slinking along the inky shadows away from the floodlight's beam. Finn kept close behind, following her lead with an ease she didn't expect from the headstrong man. Yet what Navi realized after having worked with him over this past week was that Finn made an incredible soldier. If his talents were put to proper use, he followed orders intuitively and in most situations could predict the course of action she took without her needing to utter a word. Based on the acidic comments he'd swapped with Sierra at the tavern, it had grown clear that for a while now he'd been an idling engine in his role as beta.

Every few steps or so, Navi paused, gauging the surroundings again and making sure the thrum of voices hadn't silenced and that the pounding of footsteps didn't travel in their direction. She'd slipped along the right side of the building to pad across the asphalt as she avoided loose stones and twigs with the finesse of a cat. The closer to the back of the warehouse she got, the more her nose pricked at the odd stench. Out here, shale, earth and metal were the natural ones she picked up, but as she and Finn continued their silent approach, she noted something wrong, like rotting eggs, something that made her fur stand on edge.

Back here, the doors to the warehouse were left wide open and the fumes were picked up by the breeze, the stench even stronger there. A couple of vehicles had been wheeled out back, dented pick-up trucks with the beds open and pallets piled high on each one. Navi doubted the crew here was dealing with shipping and receiving gravel and pavers like the sign out front advertised.

Headlights flicked on from the nearest truck and Navi froze.

The moment the truck rumbled their way, they'd be discovered.

The *thunk* of a few guys closing the trunk bed echoed through the clearing right when the engine of the truck roared to life. Navi didn't have time to signal to Finn — she acted on instinct. She bolted for the tall grasses surrounding the beaten dirt space here, hoping the men didn't pay attention to the shift of the shadows.

Dust clouds billowed as the truck surged forward, toward the narrow path they'd skulked down.

Navi landed in the midst of the grasses, peering out from behind the tall blades and the fringes of bushes. It wasn't until she stopped that she looked around for Finn. Her heart rammed in her chest. She searched around the clearing but didn't catch a glimpse of silver and russet fur or the glint of his amber eyes. Navi padded back and forth, trying to sneak a better view past the surrounding grasses, unable to quell the icy fear that, so used to operating on her own, she'd left her own mate to danger.

A gentle nip to her ear caused her to whip around, fangs bared.

Finn crouched behind her, his eyes glowing with warmth when he nudged her in the side. Her heartbeat returned to a reasonable rate despite the jolt of adrenaline coursing through her veins. She let out a light huff, unwilling to show how much she'd grown attached to him in such a short time.

The truck's beams filtered over them as it made the sharp turn toward the front of the warehouses and Navi ducked on instinct. Finn crouched beside her, the two of them in perfect stillness while the truck's engine whirred noisily, cutting through the soft sounds of the cicadas in the bushes and the crickets' occasional chirps. Navi didn't dare move, not wanting to alert the couple of guys who loitered in the clearing. She didn't doubt her prowess against them, but she also wasn't willing to risk letting Dale Rossi slip through her fingers.

The weight of the night out here rolled through her, the heaviness in the sticky air and the surrounding grasses laden with nature's symphony. She remained ever vigilant, watching. Waiting.

After the guys ground out their cigarettes under heel, the orange glow of the embers winking out, they headed on inside the building. Even though Finn padded back and forth a few times in impatience, Navi hadn't moved an inch, not until their footsteps transitioned to the front of the warehouse. She stepped out from the thicket of grass and bushes they'd hidden behind. At a normal place, she'd be concerned about any shifters in the group picking up their scent — however, with the meth operation in here, their nostrils would be singed by proximity.

Navi quickened her pace, veering away from the trucks as she padded in the direction of the open doors and the smog filtering out from them. They must have the meth operation running at full steam to move product fast. These warehouses might be in the boonies, but the cops around here didn't have much to entertain them — it was a matter of time before their shoestring facility got busted and shut down. If the Landsliders hadn't gotten involved in this production, Navi would've left this matter to the human police.

However, if busting their operation brought her even a step closer to finding where Mackey Kendricks had gone, the risk would be worth it.

Together, they approached the exit of the warehouse, the clouds of smog and gut-wrenching stench making her eyes water and her sensitive nose tingle. One glimpse of the facility's interior was all she needed, enough so they could set up a plan of attack. The closer they got, the more bile rose in her throat and she fought back a gag.

The warehouses lights were dimmed, with a couple of the front overheads beaming their fluorescent light down. From where she peered in, she could only spot rows of granite pavers in every shape and size as well as pallets of equipment to be shipped. It looked like the warehouse maintained a solid front as a shipping facility, if anyone was dense enough to not catch the foul stench on the breeze from the meth lab they'd slapped together. Oily sludge stained the aluminum siding and the smog drifted to cloud around the lights.

With the fluorescents beaming down in the front of the warehouse, they didn't have a hope or prayer of sneaking up to where the crew of five guys loitered. The percolating meth stripped her senses, so she couldn't even gauge if they were shifters or human. If she were dealing with any shifter crew but the Landsliders, discovery wasn't a concern. She would compel them to freeze and proceed from there. However, with the way the Landsliders had resisted her compulsion before, she couldn't bank on the ability now.

Navi tilted her head before leading Finn deeper past the lines of shelving and further away from those bright lights. Inside the warehouse, the stench intensified, but it wasn't until she followed the trail of smog that she noticed the makeshift vents protruding from the ground that poured out the noxious fumes, coming from an underground room.

She padded towards the end of the shelving before peering down in both directions. To the left, more and more stacks of boxes and crates sprawled across the warehouse until the shelves stopped to open up into a cleared front section where a couple of cranes and Bobcats sat. To the right, shadows swallowed the area. The ink-stain darkness betrayed depth and she took a few steps toward the shifting miasma, trying to distinguish what hid there.

Smoke trickled up from the scorched shadows and the stench grew so strong she could barely focus. Her eyes stung in the wake of the fumes wafting through this place and she'd already lost the ability to smell anything but the oil-thick, repulsive stench. This was indeed the site of the operation, but she had yet to spot the boss. As she approached, the slope of stairs grew more visible—this was the way to the warehouse's basement.

Even though her sense of smell had become temporarily scorched away, her hearing hadn't dulled in the slightest. So the creak of the basement door caught her attention before the spill of light from the bottom of the steps followed.

Navi's feet moved on reflex right when a man appeared at the bottom of the stairwell. The splash of sallow light from the basement revealed a sour face, wisps of black covering his shining pate, and red-rimmed eyes.

Finn wasn't moving along with her. He crouched there, fangs bared and stock still.

Fuck. No doubt, this bastard was Rossi.

Navi leapt in Finn's direction as the steps creaked and the murderer of Finn's parents ascended. She could compel Finn to follow her, but that would break the beautiful trust between them, because certain actions couldn't be revoked. Even the thought of using compulsion against her mate made her skin crawl. Navi nudged him in the side a few times, strong and urgent taps. Finn whipped around, as if her touch had jarred him from the paralysis. She tilted her head in the direction of the back door.

Creak, creak.

He was coming closer. They needed to scram, and fast.

Navi's heartbeat accelerated, adrenaline flooding through her while she bolted past the loaded shelves as quietly as possible. The guys up front wouldn't catch her scent, but if they were shifters, they had advanced hearing, too. Finn followed close behind despite the tension she could feel brimming off him.

The steps pounded louder. If Rossi happened to glance down the rows of shelving, he'd be able to spot the panther and wolf who didn't belong there.

"Hey, boss," one of the guys called from the front. The crew remained in their cluster up there, no one stepping in their direction or glancing to the shadows. Their mistake. Navi didn't waste time. They needed to leave now or risk blowing their cover. Without another glance, Navi slipped through the back door leading to the gravel lot. She landed on all fours without a sound and prowled toward the tall grasses. Her ears pricked to attention as she tensed, prepared for shouts, the clatter of footsteps or any other indicator she needed to bolt.

Finn loped past her, his eyes gleaming amber while he emanated a powder keg of tension. Together, they raced for his Challenger.

Clouds of dust filtered behind her and the pads of her feet barely touched the ground with the speed she flew forward. From the warehouse came the slow murmur of voices, even though the scent of the cooking meth clung to her fur like an oily film. The stench made her want to gag, and she had the feeling it wouldn't be leaving her any time soon.

Finn reached the Challenger before she did, and he had already begun to transform back to two feet by the time she skidded to a halt. Navi let out a breath to focus as she embraced the prickling beginning of the shift, even though her panther grumbled its disapproval, same as it always did. Out of her two forms, the ancient panther spirit would always be the more powerful and begrudge accepting the weaker one. Still, Navi was a stubborn sonofabitch.

Her claws morphed into fingernails, her fur mutated to skin and she rose on two feet again. Even with the shift, the noxious scent of the meth still stung with each inhale. She wrinkled her nose and hopped into the passenger side of Finn's Challenger. He sat in the driver's seat with his keys in the ignition and the engine thrumming. He stared ahead with a turbulent look in his eyes, his mouth forming a tight line.

"Let's head out, Finn," Navi said, her voice level and quiet.

His dark gaze flashed and he slammed his hands against the steering wheel. "Fuck, fuck, fuck," he roared, the sound reverberating through the car. Beneath the intense anger brimming off him was a grief so raw it twisted her chest. This deep sorrow belonged to a boy who'd found his parents murdered. Who had experienced far too much, too early. She could relate. Navi didn't say a word in response, just let him process the torrent that rushed through him fierce as a hurricane.

He jammed on the gas pedal and the Challenger shot off down the road. Finn's anger didn't dissipate and his aggression heated the space between them. Navi would never rob him of that, never try to bury the rage he deserved to feel, the sort that had lit her up from the inside on too many nights to count.

Navi reached over and placed a hand on his bare thigh. He flinched at first, the touch a shock from the turmoil rocking him. He glanced to her, those umber eyes softening for a heartbeat and, in that moment, she held more power than she'd ever wielded as a member of the Tribe.

"You will avenge them," she murmured. "I swear to you his crimes will not go unpunished."

"I know." Finn's voice lowered, growing deadly, dangerous. "I'll be there to make sure."

Chapter Seventeen

After the shake-up of seeing Dale Rossi again for the
first time since his parents were murdered, Finn
wanted nothing more than to lose himself in a fight or
bury himself to the hilt in his mate. Except he needed
to drop her off to report in to the other Tribe members
holed away at the Dusty Pines Motel. Tomorrow night,
they'd be storming the warehouse and busting the
meth operation wide open. Tomorrow night, he'd pay
Rossi back for stealing away the hope that his folks
would change for the better.

Instead, they'd died as the out-of-their-mind junkies
he'd dealt with throughout his whole childhood.

Finn revved his engine, tearing across the highway in
the direction of his gym. If he made the mistake of
heading to Beaver Tavern, his mouth would get him
into more trouble tonight. He was in a mean mood and,
with the bitter way his chest burned, he needed to get
the aggression out by his lonesome for once.

Thankfully he had a gym filled with sturdy punching bags for that.

Once his gym came into view, the familiar white plaster building doused him with the first ounce of relief since he'd dropped Navi off.

At least, until he spotted the Honda Civic in his parking lot.

Because he couldn't catch a goddamn break tonight.

Finn wheeled his Challenger into the unpaved parking lot, his headlights gliding over the front steps of his building where someone sat waiting for him. His heart pinched tight in his chest and at once he found it harder to breathe. Not now. Of all times, why now? He held himself together by a thread, one step away from implosion, and Raven sat on the doorstep of his gym, the one encounter guaranteed to push him over the edge.

He placed his car into Park and shut off the engine before resting his forehead against the steering wheel. He should've tried to pull himself together and headed to Dusty Pines with Navi for the night. The woman's presence created the calm to his frenzy. Except, he had known this conversation was coming the moment the bond solidified, even if he had wanted to avoid this talk at all costs.

Hell, if he were being honest with himself, this conversation had been years and years in the making.

Finn slunk out of his car, the slam of his door echoing through the quiet clearing. Each footstep in her direction sounded too loud despite the distant peal of the cicadas and the low trickle of a distant creek. Each breath grew too heavy as he sucked down the humidity-laden air of late August. Raven didn't make any move to approach, perched on the front step of his gym.

Blood pounded through his veins with such an intense demand he was tempted to walk right past her and go slam his fists into some punching bags. Her chocolate eyes were dull, and she hunched over with a lost, hopeless look that tugged at his guilt. She ran a hand through her thick, glossy strands, still wearing her normal bartending getup of a black tank-top and thigh-length skirt. No way she hadn't heard the racket he'd kicked up on approach, but she didn't glance his way once.

Each step forward served to remind him of how much history they shared. All the insecurities that had gripped him for so long and all the times he'd deluded himself into thinking their complicated relationship worked filled him with so much loathing he could taste it on his tongue. In the wake of his connection with Navi and the steady sense of right she provided, his tangled mess of a past with Raven rang all the hollower.

Finn came to a halt in front of her, hooking his thumbs through the belt loops of his jeans. "So, I'm guessing you heard the news." Guilt thrummed through him that he hadn't been the one to break it to her. With all the hustle he'd been swept up in, Finn had allowed that conversation to slip out of his grasp.

Her lips thinned, but she didn't respond. He'd tried to warn her when he first hooked up with Navi. Finn had tried to get her to stand on her own two feet and ditch her futile hope of a future they'd never have. Not like his attempt had worked. No matter what, Rae would always use him as an excuse, a crutch. And he'd had enough of both of their excuses and self-deception to last a lifetime.

Her lack of a response unsettled him and, on top of that, her grief weighted the air. Yet he couldn't help the conflicting annoyance always marring his sympathy with her situation, brought on by the way she refused to listen to him. Raven had grown more and more lost in her fantasies over the years to the point where she'd argue any point or suggestion that contradicted them.

"Just because you think she's your mate doesn't mean she's the one you'll end up with," Raven murmured. "Are you willing to throw away everything you have here? Everything we've shared?" Her dark eyes glittered while she continued to delude herself even now, ignoring the irrevocable truth. They weren't meant to be. Her dismissal of Navi rubbed him raw.

"And what do I have here, Rae?" he shot back. "An alpha who barely needs me and a toxic as hell relationship I should have quit years ago? Navi is mine, and I don't give a fuck if you refuse to accept our bond. This isn't your decision to make. It never was."

She flinched at his rejection. Her hands curled into fists in her lap, and she sat there, shoulders bowed, like she was still sixteen and seeking comfort from one hellish childhood. This close to her, he couldn't help but remember how they'd clashed together over the years, two kids trying to bury their pain in each other. Yet his attraction to Raven had faded long ago and it was a dim bulb compared to the sun's glow Navi provided.

For the first time, Finn wasn't avoiding his problems or his past. Navi encouraged him to conquer them and she inspired him to fight in a way no one else had before.

"What sort of future do you think you can find with a Tribe member?" she argued, venom in her voice as her nails lengthened to claws. "As soon as she's wrapped up here, she'll be heading to the next town to find someone new."

Her words twisted inside him and Finn couldn't help the heat burning in his chest. "What makes you think I'm staying here?"

When those words left him, Raven's eyes widened and she stopped cold. He and Navi had yet to have the conversation, but, as he spoke it, the inevitability of the situation settled in his gut. In choosing her, he would be leaving his home behind.

"You wouldn't," she whispered, rising from her perch on the step. Tears glittered in her eyes, and he couldn't help the turmoil that raged through him, the toxic combination of guilt, anger and always sadness for Raven.

"She's my mate, Rae. My future," Finn responded, his words coming out softer with the wonder of what he'd found in Navi. Several drops slithered down Raven's cheeks, illuminated by the silver of the moon. His chest squeezed tight as he kept his hand back. Any other time, he would've reached over and brushed the tears away, but she needed to find a new source of comfort. He hoped she would be able to summon that strength within herself.

Finn was winning the award for world's biggest asshole tonight, but he needed to let her process this on her own, the same as he had some work to do on a punching bag in his gym. He met her eyes, staring at the tears without flinching and without caving to the guilt and pain that had torn him up for so long.

"You will survive without me, Rae," he said, his throat tightening with the words. "You've got a bright and brilliant future out there, I know it. You just have to be brave enough to reach for it." Even as he spoke those words, he knew they weren't only for her. After all, he'd been restless here for far too long, terrified to move past this place after the hell his parents put him through the first time he'd separated from the Red Rock pack.

She shook her head before storming past him.

Finn didn't follow, just made his way to the door of Kelly's Gym. The engine revved from her Honda, and those headlights sliced fluorescent beams through the darkness of the lot. Within seconds, Raven pulled out of her spot and accelerated down the highway. His grip on the handle tightened when she disappeared out of sight.

The mounting aggression that had burned through him earlier had been strangled in the wake of his confrontation with Raven. Finn entered the room, the scent of sweat heavy in the air, as well as the lingering remnants of apple and vanilla, an aroma that shot straight to his cock. Finn ran a hand across his buzz cut, trying to ignore the droplets of sweat tickling while they coursed down his neck to soak into his T-shirt.

He flicked on the overhead lights, but even the bright fluorescents didn't stand a chance at dispelling the loneliness that waited for him in the creeping shadows and the silence. He swallowed, hard, as he grabbed his bandage to wrap his fists before approaching the punching bag.

Finn settled himself in front of the black Everlast bag, his shoulders dropping as he prepared to sling his punches.

One. Two. His fists shot out, hitting the weight in succession.

Raven's tears wouldn't leave his mind. The pit in his chest widened.

He lunged forward, delivering another couple of raps to the bag. Finn stepped back, moving side to side while he tried to shake off the emotional storm that promised to devastate him.

The years hadn't been kind to Dale Rossi, but those soulless eyes had held the same malevolence Finn remembered from the motel. The same detached expression he'd never forget.

One. Two. One. Two. His shoulders heaved up and down as he lobbed punch after punch into the bag. Drops of sweat flew to the mats and the chain holding the bag rattled as it swung violently, but he kept pounding away. Because if he stopped, those memories would win. If he stopped, his mind would take him to dark places he'd believed he'd escaped from long ago. His fists blurred, his knuckles throbbed, yet his chest remained in a tight vise while he struggled to suck in his breaths.

All he could taste was the oily air of the meth lab. All he could see was the blood splattered around the motel.

Smack, smack, smack. The wet thwacks of his flesh pounding against the bag gave him pause. His claws pricked out, shredding through the gauze he'd wrapped around his fists. Droplets of blood mingled with the sweat hitting the floor and trickled from his hands.

"Fuck," he cursed, his shoulders heaving up and down as he panted, staring at the weighted bag and ready to go another couple of rounds. He wanted to hurt tonight, wanted to forget the anger on Sierra's face and the upset on Raven's as his mouth ran away with his anger and started pissing off people he gave a damn about.

A creak sounded from the door to his gym, causing Finn to tense.

"Raven, I told you no," he called out before he turned around.

Except the scent at the door soothed him in a way no one else could.

"And what was Raven doing here?" Navi's voice broke through the quiet of the room. As she approached, slinking forward with those lethal curves despite her short stature, her eyes glowed silver. In their mating frenzy, emotions were running high and hot, yet he'd tackled the conversation with Raven by his lonesome tonight. Not like he had much choice.

Finn's heart ached at the sight of Navi, as if her presence provided a salve to the turbulence slicing him apart on the inside.

"She was waiting for me when I got here," Finn said, unable to ignore the pulse of his heart when he approached. Navi cocked an eyebrow, percolating with silent tension. He understood — with all the things he and Navi needed to discuss, their relationship was too new and too fragile to introduce volatile elements from the past.

"Is that so?" Navi murmured, reaching out to place a hand on his chest. The heat of her palm soaked into him, offering a brief respite from the way his chest ached. "How did that conversation go?" She brimmed with as much tension as he felt and the brief flash of vulnerability in her eyes slayed him on the spot. From what he'd learned of her, Navi had been given very few choices in her life and the role of Tribe was a heavy burden. For her to choose him, for her to want this humbled him.

Finn let out a snort. "Horribly, like I screwed up every damn conversation I had today. If the Red Rock pack doesn't think I'm the biggest asshole on the planet, I only need to run into one or two more and my job is done. I can't seem to do anything but piss people off right now."

A smile rolled to her sensual lips. "You? Run your mouth? Color me shocked."

He couldn't help himself, and he wrapped his hands around her waist, drawing her close to him. Her nose wrinkled as she glanced down.

"Did you cut yourself?" she asked, reaching for his hands. The gauze had grown soaked at this point and he'd left a few stains on her shirt in the process. A line furrowed between her brows as she scanned over the spots of blood. "What the hell were you doing?" she asked, her voice soft with concern. Her hazel eyes stripped him down, as if his defenses no longer existed.

"I got a little carried away with the punching bag," Finn admitted, unable to look away from her. "It's been a day."

Navi's grip tightened around his wrist and she tugged him forward. He followed her as she led him to the closet of a bathroom in the back of his gym. She didn't say a word while they marched to the sink, but she didn't have to. As she turned the faucets on and began unwrapping the stained gauze from his hands, the tenderness in her motions said everything.

The water ran red, but already the cuts were healing. He couldn't fathom how humans lived, waiting days to weeks for slices and gouges to mend. Still, the way Navi took care of him pierced through all the chaos of his emotions and his mind. Despite the shaky ground he stood on with the Red Rocks and how his memories besieged him at the sight of his old enemy, the discovery of his mate was the one thing he didn't question.

Finn shook the remaining water off his hands before drying them with a nearby towel. "Looks like I ruined your shirt," he commented, scanning over the stain he'd left. His gaze lingered on the swell of her breasts and the curve of her hips, on the smooth skin he longed to sink his teeth into. She'd tasted honey sweet this morning and the way she'd come undone on the hood of his Challenger would be the fodder of his fantasies for a long time to come.

Navi's mouth quirked as she fought a smile. She tugged the shirt over her head, the fabric hitting the ground with a soft thump. "Guess I'll have to do away with it."

She wasn't wearing a bra. Finn took in a sharp breath, because his cock rose to attention at the sight of her bare breasts. Her dark nipples were stiff, small points he wanted to suck, tease and nip, and the perfect curve of her soft breasts banished any other thought from his mind. He wanted to bury himself inside her.

"Look," she said, tapping his chin up until their eyes met. "I know we've both had one mindfuck of a day and there's a lot we need to discuss. But right now, my mind isn't a place I want to be. I need you, Finn."

Like she needed to say anything else. Finn crossed the space between them, grabbed her by the waist and kissed Navi Tremere with everything he had.

Chapter Eighteen

The moment Finn's mouth touched hers, Navi banished all worries of the day — of the upcoming meth lab bust, of their undiscussed future and of how Raven's scent lingered in this place. Today had been hellish, joyous and terrifying all in one gasp. He tightened his grip around her hips and she surrendered to how her body sparked to life at his touch. At the way he made her feel like she was freefalling yet standing on solid ground all at the same time.

He circled his hands around her waist and hoisted her up. She wrapped herself around his hips, pressing the hard length of him against her, making her core pulse in return. The sensitive tips of her nipples brushed against the fabric of his shirt, sending a jolt through her. This close, the air heated between them, and a film of sweat caused his skin to glisten. She leaned into the crook of his neck, sinking her teeth into the slope. He tasted like salt and sweat and he dug his fingers into her hips in response.

"I need you inside me, now," she murmured, brushing her lips against his skin. She ached for him with an intensity that defied reason. Beyond that, though, she couldn't admit she was scared. She was terrified of the depth of her feelings for him and how the brief time they'd spent apart had brought all those fears crashing down until she could barely breathe. They'd never discussed anything, and he owed her nothing.

When this case came to a close, he could decide to stay with the Red Rocks and yet she would always have to leave. Always. The thought caused her throat to tighten and she pressed herself even closer to him, as if the skin-on-skin contact might banish those dizzying fears.

Finn carried her across the room as though she weighed nothing. His absolute fearlessness with her was something she cherished. Too many times, others veered away due to her power, and the distance she'd accumulated over the years made connecting even harder and trusting difficult. So she remained in control, always. Yet when it came to Finn and the sheer passion he leveled at her, Navi couldn't help but surrender.

He lowered her onto the weight bench in the back of the room and undid the latch on his belt. A hunger squeezed her chest tight, and she reached out to grab his zipper and tug it down with a snick. Navi slid to her knees in front of him while he shucked his pants to the ground, boxer-briefs too. His cock was stark in the air in front of her and she licked her lips as she glanced to him. The heated look in his deep brown eyes, the singular focus made her feel like she was the only one in his universe.

God, I need that right now.

Navi dipped forward to take the velvet length of him in her mouth. His hot, hard cock tensed as she began to suck. The groan that came out of him made her pussy pulse and wetness pooled between her thighs when she inhaled the scent of him, all leather and sweat. He ran fingers through her hair, thrusting his hips forward with an eagerness that didn't surprise her. Finn Kelly threw the entirety of himself into everything he did.

His cock stiffened in her mouth, and his thighs tensed. Finn gripped the strands of her hair tighter, pulling her back. "You've got me so fucking horny I'm liable to blow," he said, stepping away. "I want to come inside you."

She slunk toward him to trail the tip of her tongue on the underside of his erection, tasting the pre-cum on the head. Finn let out a low curse and grabbed her hand, tugging her up from her crouch. Navi slipped her finger underneath his shirt and pulled the hem up as he helped her toss it over his head. She shimmied out of her shorts, enjoying the way Finn's eyes blazed when she slipped her panties down to follow.

"Turn around, now," he growled, his feral side coming to life in a way that made her panther purr. She complied, standing in front of the weight bench, and the delicious idea made her ache for him all the more.

He pressed himself against her, his rock-hard chest to her back, and he brushed his stiff cock against her ass. The feel of him made her core clench, made every ounce of her tune to awareness at how badly she needed to be filled by him. How she needed to banish her fears tonight. She dipped down to place her palms on the weight bench in front of her, grinding her ass against his cock. He ran his hands up her thighs, tracing the path of the tattoos emblazoned on her skin.

"You're perfect," Finn said, the words slipping out in such a quiet hush that she almost didn't hear them. The emotion behind them made her throat tight and her eyes burned at the thought that this might be their last time together. The possibility of going their separate ways after finding something so brilliant and true tore her to shreds.

He brushed the tip of his cock against her drenched folds, the sensation rushing through her in a fierce sweep. Finn settled his big palms around her hips, the heat soaking through as he made her feel small and feminine in a way she never had before. He nudged his head in and she tilted her hips up to accept more of him inside her. As he lowered his length into her, she let out a low moan at the sweep of relief prickling through her arms and legs.

Finn settled inside her and she let out a gasp at the delicious way he filled her to the hilt. This, this was what she needed. Once he rocked his hips, moving his length in and out of her, every worry, concern and fear vanished. Navi sank into the rhythm of the way he drove into her, how each time she ground her sensitive clit against him she saw stars. She curled her nails into the tough fabric of the weight bench and sweat pooled beneath her palms.

Navi cried out at the pleasure flowing through her, at the increased pace while he fucked her harder, faster and with the ferocious edge she needed. Both of them moved with the fury of desperation, trying to abandon the turmoil plaguing them. Finn had worn his damage on his face clear as day when they'd left the meth shack and she'd been haunted ever since they'd become mated. Navi should've left him alone to his thoughts tonight, but she needed him as badly as he did her.

She didn't want to quit him. She didn't want to leave him behind.

The slight sting of the slap of skin when they slammed together sent a thrill through her veins. His name was a prayer on her lips as he edged her closer and closer. They moved with the frenzy of abandon, and Navi sank into the bliss of their dance. Her mind blanked as she surrendered to the sensations pulsing through her from the scent of him, all leather and sweat to the bite of his grip around her hips. Her clit tingled from the frenetic pace, sensitized and enhancing every collision. Her pussy clenched. *So, so, close.*

He thrust into her, hot, hard and filling her to entirety. As he collided with her, Finn leaned down to sink his teeth into her shoulder. The bite pushed her over the edge.

Molten pleasure rushed through her in a torrent and her core squeezed tight, pulsing with the throes of her orgasm. Navi cried out, right as his cock kicked inside her, heat flooding through. Her legs trembled while she came, but Finn's grip on her didn't falter. He leaned over her, his big body near crushing her, but she didn't want to move. Didn't want to leave the safety of his embrace. For the first time she understood why Akio fought to keep his mate on the road with him and why he braved those fights and the fears. Because this connection was one worth fighting for.

Sweat pricked her forehead as she sagged against the weight bench and her body grew loose in the wake of the intense orgasms that racked through her. If she could stay like this forever, she would, with his heavy weight on her, skin to skin and connected in the deepest way possible. Except, this had been a temporary avoidance of their very real problems.

Slowly, Finn pulled himself out of her and rose. Navi still sagged over the weight bench, not ready to face the day. A second later, he wrapped those muscular arms around her and heaved her up with little effort.

"Come on," he said, slipping her into his arms to carry her across the room.

Navi lifted a brow with an amused smile. "Ready to kick me out already?"

Finn shot a glare at her. "What gave you that idea? We're not sleeping in my gym, so you're coming to my place so we can crash out in a real bed."

"Help, help, I'm being kidnapped," Navi murmured in a dry tone. She reached up to flick her fingers against his abs. His brows wrinkled at the feeble attempt. "Oh well," she continued, unable to hide the hint of a grin on her lips. "Didn't work. I suppose I'll resign myself to my horrible fate."

Finn snorted. He didn't bother grabbing their scattered clothes as he made his way to the door. "That's right, the big bad wolf is dragging you off to his den of torment. The horrors of sleeping in a real bed instead of on sweaty gym mats."

Navi watched, impressed, as he leaned down with her still in his arms to grab his keys from the latch. "You want to be giving the roadside a show?" she asked, glancing to their discarded clothing.

Finn reached for the knob and nudged the door open. "They saw plenty earlier," he murmured, a boyish grin lifting his lips. She couldn't help how her heart pounded in double time at the sight. The cooler night air coated her skin and he clutched her tighter to his chest when he leaned down to lock his door. The roadside remained empty, though Navi was well aware of the floodlight illuminating this lot. She could slip out and walk on her own, but she didn't want to admit she loved Finn's overabundance of affection.

He stopped in front of his Challenger and lowered her to the ground. "I'm just up the road, so we can get some shut-eye there. We can scandalize all the neighbors on the way."

Navi couldn't resist her smile and she lifted her arms to skim her fingers across his buzz cut even though he had to duck his head for her to reach. "I'm sure you achieve that enough all by your lonesome."

He slipped his hands around her waist, drawing her close. As she looked into his eyes, a tenderness emanating from them that she'd never experienced to this degree, a shiver rolled down her spine. Navi had spent a lifetime keeping people at a distance and had learned her lesson early on that she'd never be able to sustain any real friendships or connections with a life on the road, apart from with the other members of the Tribe. And even with them, they all acted as sole operators so often it never quite felt like the togetherness of a pack.

Navi swallowed the lump in her throat, sending a silent prayer to the Great Spirits. For once in her life, if she wanted to defy the past and hold on to someone — she wanted to keep Finn Kelly.

* * * *

When Navi woke up, she almost leapt out of the bed, fangs bared. This wasn't her shared room in the Dusty Pines Motel and she didn't recognize her surroundings in the slightest. Sunlight spilled out of broad windows that faced the surrounding forest and at least a dozen half-open books lay scattered around the floor along with piles of folded clothes and an over-full hamper. Thick, rumpled sheets surrounded her like a cocoon. As she breathed in, Finn's familiar scent brought back memories of the night before.

Except he wasn't anywhere in the room.

Rustling came from farther into the house. Navi slipped out of the bed and snagged one of his oversized, rumpled tees to toss on. If he didn't like her stealing his clothes, it served him right for abandoning hers at the gym last night. They'd begun making out the moment they slipped into his bed, but exhaustion had claimed them fast. His heavy weight against her as she'd fallen asleep and the lull of his steady breathing — all that came with sleeping beside someone was a foreign experience for her, one she cherished.

Without a sound, she stepped out of his bedroom and farther into his apartment. Darkness shrouded the main room at the end of the hall, though she could make out some silver weights on the floor, a couch and loveseat with black slipcovers on them and a stout hardwood coffee table in the center of the room. To her left, bright light spilled from another room — if she had to hazard a guess, the kitchen.

Navi stepped through the cream doorframe to the kitchen in time for Finn to whirl around in her direction. He wore a loose pair of shorts, the luscious, tan abs on full display, and he carried two mugs in his hands, steam curling up from the piping hot liquid. His brows shot up in surprise and he almost lost his grip. The way he scanned her over, as though he wanted to lick her head to toe, had her core clenching.

"Hey, stranger," she murmured, reaching out for the cup of coffee. The warmth of the mug printed on her palms. "You can't be for real. Already up and coffee made?"

Finn broke into a smile that crinkled around his eyes. Her heart sped at the sight of him and she couldn't help the desperate, dizzying affection that rushed through her.

"What can I say?" he responded. "I'm one of those mythical morning people." He leaned against the bamboo countertop in his kitchen. The pure white cabinets behind him made his sunkissed skin glow, as if he could get more attractive. His gaze landed square on her. "If I had it my way, you'd be wearing my shirts every day. You look fuckable as hell, babe."

Navi couldn't help the heat rising to her cheeks at the compliment, or the earnest affection in his eyes. This, the simplicity of having morning coffee the night after amazing sex, was something so many took for granted. If someone had told her years ago she'd be standing here, across from her mate, she would've laughed in their face. Navi never stayed the night—waste of time and she didn't have room in her heart for more broken memories.

Which is why they needed to have a serious conversation. Because if this was goodbye—if Finn remained here—she wasn't sure if she could ever glue her shattered pieces together again.

She lifted the coffee to her mouth and took a sip, her own brand of liquid courage. As the hot fluid slipped down her throat, she stood a little straighter. "We haven't had a chance to talk yet," she said, feeling as though she was stepping onto the precipice of a ledge, ready to drop into a canyon below. The coziness of the morning and the scorching memories of last night began to gray around the edges in the wake of the fear threatening to steal her breath away. Finn's brows furrowed and his frown made her feel queasy.

"What's there to talk about?" he asked, gripping tight to the counter. "We're mated and you've got another thing coming if you think you can start throwing up barriers and excuses. Don't tell me you already got tired of me." Even though his tone remained lighthearted, the troubled way his dark eyes shone was anything but.

"I can't stay here, Finn," she said, unable to hide the pleading in her voice. She tried another sip of coffee, but even the heat couldn't dispel the arctic depths her core plummeted to. "I'm Tribe. I have to go where I'm called."

"When did I ask you to?" His voice softened. He crossed the tiles between them and plucked her coffee from her hands to put the mug on the countertop. When he faced her again, all reason abandoned her. Every logical word on her tongue melted away. She wanted him. She wanted him with a passion she'd never allowed herself to have before, with a longing so intense she almost buckled from the weight.

He tilted her chin up so she couldn't look away and the tenderness in his eyes broke her. Fuck, fuck, fuck. She was terrified of asking, terrified of the rejection, but if anyone was worth the leap, it was Finn. As one of the Tribe, she made the ultimate choice, not him.

"Would you come with me?" she asked, unable to hide the tremble in her voice. She hated the weakness and vulnerability, but everything about this situation stripped her raw. Her tongue dried while she waited for a response, barely able to suck in another breath. It took until now, but she'd put the words out there.

Now to see if she'd shatter to pieces.

"I was wondering when you'd ask," he murmured back with a soft smile. He ran his thumb across her lower lip. "Navi, once we became mates, there was no other option—not in my mind. You've got to be crazy if you think I'd let you slip out of my hands after finding you."

Heat seared her eyes and she inhaled a shaky breath. Relief crashed through her in such a fierce tidal wave her lip trembled. Only for a moment, but Finn leaned down to place a kiss on her lips, filling her with the heat of him, the solid strength of him and the steadying, grounding force that had become an addiction. This must be a dream, had to be some fantasy she'd cooked up, because never in a thousand years had she believed she could have this sort of future.

His arms wrapped around her and, even as their kiss ended, she rested her head against his bare chest. "What about your position as beta?" Navi asked, murmuring against his skin. "We don't have anything like that for you on the road."

Finn squeezed her tighter to him and she basked in the touch hunger claiming them both. "Don't know if you noticed, but my position as Sierra's right-hand man got complicated the moment Dax came into the equation."

Guilt tugged at her heart—she'd never asked for a life on the road and she understood how disruptive that path could be. She didn't want to inflict that on someone she cared about. "When are you going to break the news?" she asked.

He pressed a kiss onto her head, still holding on to her like a lifeline. Despite the way he reassured her, he waded through as much unknown territory as she did and, on top of that, he was preparing to leave the only home he'd ever known. How he emanated so much calm baffled her.

"After we launch the attack against Dale Rossi and his men," Finn said, his voice growing deeper, darker. "One challenge at a time."

Navi nodded, pulling away from him to steady herself. She matched his unwavering gaze, the feral side of her peering out with the fight they were gearing up for. "Tonight, you'll finish off Dale Rossi for good."

Chapter Nineteen

Finn was going to face the man who'd murdered his parents tonight and he would claim his revenge.

After Navi left his place, he headed over to his gym, seeking the comfort of familiarity while he had it. Finn breathed in the scents of sweat, of the metal weights and of the overused canvas mats. As the breath filled his chest, he snapped a kick out, his shin thudding against the same punching bag that had met his aggressions the night before.

The door to his gym opened with a creak. Finn's shoulders tensed. He needed to start locking up behind him.

On a normal day, he'd relax at the sight of his alpha, but with the news he needed to break to her and how their last conversation had gone, this talk would be as pleasant as gargling with Drano. To top it off, he couldn't rid himself of the memories brewing in his brain, ones that coated his skin like a film he wanted to scrub off. Finn rolled his shoulders back and began to unwrap his hands, the sweat gluing the bandages together. Sierra slunk forward with lupine grace and he couldn't deny his kinship with this woman, the sister he'd always wanted. No matter how they clashed, he couldn't erase the respect for her forged through the years.

"I'm joining the hunt tonight," Sierra said, breaking through the silence between them. "Navi and the others gave me the heads-up." She picked up one of the hand weights and pumped it, focusing on the movement. He didn't want to face the awkwardness that settled between them either.

Finn grabbed another weight from the line-up and joined her. If he could burn some of the anger and energy roiling through him, it would be better for everyone. "Dale Rossi's mine," he muttered, unable to form the words to broach the topic of leaving. Hell, when he'd agreed to go with her this morning, he had barely thought of anything beyond the thrill Navi sent through him and how he couldn't let this go, no matter what.

Leaving didn't just mean no more pints at Beaver Tavern, poker games with Jer, skinny dipping with Raven and sparring with Sierra. He'd have to close the gym he'd built from scratch, find a way to do sessions on the road or work freelance. He'd built so much here over the years — a home, a business and a life. Except, no matter how many memories warmed his bones, he knew deep in his gut, no part of him could build a future here.

"I'm leaving with her." The words slipped from him without a second thought. He hadn't intended to state the news so bluntly and he'd hoped to hash out their issues before dropping the blow, but Finn had never been one for subtlety or tact.

Sierra paused mid-curl and rested her dark gaze on him. "I know."

Finn's brows furrowed as he lifted a heavier weight and set to work. "How? I just told Navi this morning."

Her gaze held an understanding he didn't expect, the wisdom the Red Rock alpha was known for. "I knew the moment you told me she was your mate, Finn," Sierra murmured, her smile not reaching her eyes. "You can't hide your emotions for shit. You've never been able to and I'm disappointed in myself that it took me this long to see how unhappy you've been here."

Finn shrugged, the uncomfortableness of her admission prickling across his skin. "You've been occupied and rightfully so. On top of the normal load you have on your shoulders, you were balancing a new mate and integrating his pack into the fold. With all these seismic changes to the pack, though, my place got lost along the way." Finn placed his weight down and turned to face her. "You don't need me anymore, Sierra—at least, not the way you did."

She pressed her lips tight together and he watched how she swallowed, rather than saying anything. The proud as hell woman wouldn't cry in front of him, but he could feel the crash of that sadness as it descended.

Sierra's eyes flashed amber, the familiar color of her wolf, one his own had responded to all these years. "Don't discredit yourself, Kelly," she said, cuffing his shoulder. "No one happens to call me on my shit like you do. However, I also know I can't keep you here. I've been so wrapped up in Dax and the changes to the pack I overlooked one of the most important members."

Finn's throat tightened and — he wasn't going to lie to himself — his eyes heated. He'd met Sierra when she had arrived in the pack, a quiet, sharp and lethal teen, and he'd been all bluster and flames. Over the years, she'd become more confident, louder and grown into a person he couldn't help but respect. He was still bluster and flames, stuck in the same spin cycle he'd been repeating since he was a kid. For the first time in his life, he would be breaking that cycle.

"Bring it on in, hardass," Finn said, wrapping his arms around Sierra in a fierce hug. His alpha was all prickles and quills, her care delivered through actions rather than any touch. That was one of the things Sierra and Navi shared. "I might be leaving, but it's not like you won't ever see me again. This will always be the place where I grew up and the home that shaped me. I'm sorry for breaking up the dream team."

Sierra sucked in a sharp breath and he swallowed, hard. His alpha pulled out of the hug and lifted her chin. She clapped a hand on his shoulder, the sting drawing him to the present. "Then let's make this final hunt count."

* * * *

When Finn pulled up to the Dusty Pines Motel, Navi was sitting on the front stoop with a grim expression on her face. He felt the same way, his chest gripped in a vise. Shadows coated their surroundings, but, as a wolf shifter, he'd always had a predilection for seeing things in the darkness. Night had fallen, and the time arrived faster than Finn could prepare for. They could rally the numbers to take this operation down, but if they wanted to corner the Landsliders and stamp out Rossi, they needed to keep their crew as bare bones as possible. The element of surprise was the only way they'd corner the slippery bastard.

He rolled down his window and let out a low whistle, leaning against the side. "What's a gorgeous girl like you doing by your lonesome?"

Navi shook her head with an exasperated grin as she rose from the stoop and brushed her jean shorts off. He wasn't lying, though—even in a beat-up pair of jean shorts and a ratty lavender tank top, she looked fucking sexy. She had hips made for gripping, and the sort of tits he fantasized about. She hooked her thumbs through the belt loops of her jeans while she approached.

"You can quit with the sweet-talking, Kelly. We're already mated," Navi said as she slipped into the passenger side of his Challenger. He adored the gruff exterior she clung to, how she disarmed his affection like a small smile wasn't clinging to her lips and she wasn't getting the slightest bit flustered. Based on the brief glimpses of vulnerability he'd received from her, Finn understood with pristine clarity that each of those moments was priceless.

"Can't help it—every time I see you I realize what a lucky bastard I am," he murmured, leaning in to claim her lips. Despite the way his nerves buzzed, her mouth against his soothed him. She sank against him, her kisses slow, sensual and igniting his libido on the spot.

When she pulled back, she swiped at a piece of her pixie cut and inhaled before looking at him with the serious expression he'd begun terming her 'business face.'

"I sent Jess and some of the Red Rocks and Silver Springs ahead to scout the outlying areas for

Landslider activity. We don't want anyone escaping when we launch our attack." Her tone contained the brisk efficiency he was used to from the Tribe, but when their eyes met, her gaze melted with a tenderness she only shared with him. "Are you ready to bust this meth lab wide open?" she asked.

In response, Finn revved his engine and set out from the Dusty Pines Motel with a cloud of dust behind him.

"Are things always this exciting on the jobs?" Finn asked while he set out down the highway in the direction of the warehouses. The darkness of night swallowed the pathway, and even the beams of his car fought through the murky shadows.

Navi let out a snort. "Apart from the complications involving whatever Mackey did to his Landsliders, busting up shifter meth labs is one of the tamer things I've done as part of the Tribe. Though, we're just as likely to get called into territories for mating ceremonies." The annoyance rang clear in her voice, eliciting an amused smirk from him.

"Good to know I never have to worry about being suckered into watching rom-coms with you," he responded, speeding down the highway as fast as he could. His skin itched with anticipation and he couldn't dispel his nerves at this point. His wolf lunged in his chest, desperate to hunt, to fight. Amidst all the rising aggression, illogical fear gripped him by the throat. The same fear he'd felt as a kid, waiting to be discovered by Rossi and his guys.

"I'm more of a documentary kind of gal," Navi responded.

Finn let out a gagging sound. "That's a thousand times worse."

She shrugged. "I've got to stay current on our kind — comes with the territory and they provide a great opportunity to learn, whether it's the history of shifters or how the humans are receiving us."

"I'm falling asleep at the thought of them," he retorted, unable to hide his grin. A sharp elbow met his arm a moment later.

Once those warehouse lights cropped into view, the joking ceased and they both lapsed into laden silence. Nothing could quite prepare him to face this demon from his past, but he knew he needed to try. Navi had helped him break the cycle of living in fear and given him the opportunity to claim revenge for the hope Rossi stole from him so long ago. He'd been a starved, leashed child back then, caged by parents who forgot about him at every turn, slave to their addictions.

He wasn't a kid anymore. Finn was the beta of the Red Rocks, a wolf shifter who had fought and killed for his pack and his people. Despite the damage his parents had done, he'd grown into a fighter and a survivor. And with the discovery of his mate, he had been freed from his remaining tethers. *Free to become who I was meant to be.*

The soft glow of the overhead lights grew stronger the nearer he and Navi got. His heart pounded as he pulled up to the spot along the side of the road that he'd hidden his car at before. When he switched into Park, their silence threatened to suck the air out of the car.

Headlights flashed in his rearview mirror, drawing his attention. If it was one of the Landsliders — or, hell, anyone in Rossi's entourage — the jig might be up before they ever got out of his Challenger.

The car slowed and, a moment later, pulled up behind him. He squinted, staring into the rearview. He recognized Sierra's beat-up Chevy and his shoulders sank with relief. Navi had stepped out of the passenger's side by the time he opened his door. Sierra and Jer hopped out of her car to greet them with the quiet approach of their kind. Finn walked up to Jer and clapped a hand on his shoulder in greeting, the motion reciprocated. Jer met his eyes, his mouth a grim line and understanding reflected in his gaze.

Out of anyone, Jer understood what Finn would face tonight.

As Tribe, Navi stepped into the leadership role effortlessly. "We'll approach in human form first, but the moment they put up a fight, shift." Everyone nodded in understanding. "Don't try for heroics," Navi warned. "If the situation's hot, get out. Don't give chase without letting someone else know your position." Her gaze rested on him. Not like he planned on throwing himself into the fire, but hothead that he was, if Rossi tried to escape, he knew he'd be singleminded in tracking him down.

"Let's go clean up the area," Finn murmured, his voice low and lethal. "I've got a score to settle."

Chapter Twenty

Navi's senses pricked to alert the moment she and Finn began their approach to the warehouse. Like the night before, those lights remained on, but this time, they wouldn't be sneaking around to avoid detection. This would be a confrontation of claw and fang since the easier solution of compelling them to back down wasn't in the cards. Blood would be spilled.

She turned to them when they reached the edge of the tall grasses and caught the murmur of voices from inside. "We've got to block off all the entrances — make sure none of them go running. Sierra and I will take the front to draw the crowd. Jeremiah and Finn, you head around the back to the meth lab. Don't let Rossi escape and if you happen to find any manifests or details on Mackey Kendricks and his goal with the Landsliders, he's the real target in all of this."

Navi worked her jaw, ready to turn on her heel and head out when Finn grabbed her wrist.

"Stay safe," he said, the tenderness in his umber eyes something she wasn't used to.

"If you let Rossi kill you, I'll drag you from the grave to kill you myself," she responded, her tone gruffer than normal as she wrapped her other hand over his. She wanted this moment to stretch out for as long as possible, to stay connected to him. On a normal mission she leapt in with little abandon, only worrying about staying alive. However, her heart squeezed tight at the seriousness in his eyes and the knowledge that she was sending him to fight a man who helped destroy his childhood. This change in her status quo left her feeling stripped and raw in its wake.

He leaned in to brush his lips against hers and, as fast, he slunk through the tall grasses toward the back of the warehouse where the horrible gusts from the meth lab wafted out. Jer slipped behind him quick and silent, the two of them living up to their wolfish stealth.

Navi turned to Sierra as she shook off the residual feelings sweeping through her. It was game time — just another day on the job.

"Let's go tear up some meth-dealing assholes," Navi said, flashing a grin to the Red Rock alpha. Sierra bared her fangs with a lethal smile and together they strode toward the front door. Unlike the other night, they could throw stealth to the breeze, because they were playing the distraction tonight. She might not have compulsion on her side, but on top of her panther's lethality, she had Tribe magic at her disposal, the water that flowed at her command. These Landsliders wouldn't know what hit them.

Sierra walked with a similar confidence, the alpha well trained from years of sparring and comfortable with the prospect of fighting for her territory. Out of the many alphas they'd dealt with, Navi could see why Jess liked the lady and Finn had followed her for so long. From their brief interactions, she felt a kindred spirit with the tough chick who would dive headfirst into trouble if it meant protecting her pack.

As Navi got closer to the door, those voices grew louder and she tried to tune in to figure out how many men clustered behind the front door.

"Latch the door once we get inside," Navi murmured while she stepped to the entrance. Once she rattled the doorknob, the voices quieted.

They couldn't operate on the element of surprise, but, as Tribe, she'd always have one trick in her back pocket. Her panther lashed back and forth in her chest, demanding to emerge, to tear these assholes to pieces. Navi flung the door open and strode inside. The focus of every guy in the room, all six of them, turned to her and Sierra.

Growls ripped the air from the men, and she caught more than a couple of glowing eyes out of the bunch.

"I'm Navi Tremere of the East Coast Tribe," she called out, her voice booming to the rafters of this warehouse. "You've been found guilty of smuggling and meth dealing, but if you give me information on Mackey Kendricks here and now, we can talk about easing your sentence."

The growling hadn't ceased and, with the hunched-shoulder way they regarded her, helpfulness didn't seem to be their top priority. *Their loss.*

One of the guys called back, "Kendricks is a helluva lot scarier than you. I think we'll just head out and we can call this tussle a draw, yeah?"

Sierra grinned as she stepped beside Navi. "Door's locked as requested." She scanned over the crowd with her arms crossed. "Only six guys? It's like they're asking to get taken down."

Navi snorted. "You had your warning," she called. "Now we'll be using lethal force."

She didn't wait for their response. Time for the panther to emerge. The shift took her over while the claws extended from her nails and the fur began to prick through her skin. The clothes she'd been wearing shredded to the floor. Her bones transitioned until she was on four paws instead of two feet and her panther blazed with readiness. Her fangs itched to sink into these bastards. A silver wolf with black streaks padded beside her—Sierra's form. They shared a single glance, but they didn't need communication to know what came next.

As the six men began to shift, Navi and Sierra attacked.

She lunged forward, towering over the first mangy wolf to come rushing her way. He tried to ram into her, but Navi already tilted her head down to use her thick skull like a battering ram. She met his attack with gusto, the force of her push-back sending him flying.

The shift in the air alerted her before a mountain lion leapt from the right, fangs bared.

Navi whipped toward him.

Before he could land, she swiped with one paw, claws out. The tips sank in past his fur, into flesh, and she raked down. The lion roared with pain as blood sprayed from the open wound, the tinny scent bright in the air. He pushed through the attack. A second later he slammed into her in the side, headfirst. Navi moved with the blow, soaking the abrupt disruption.

Sierra let out a low growl as a black bear and another wolf advanced on her.

Navi let out a low huff—she wasn't the only one fighting here. She needed to keep Sierra safe through this.

She gathered her powers, drawing upon the connection she shared with her panther and the gifts of the shaman bestowed upon her. The water prickled inside and she channeled her abilities to summon it from the ground, from any source around them. Quickly, the drops condensed into a stream.

The other black bear came lumbering for her.

Navi swerved out of the way like the liquid she wielded, the slow-moving creature not standing a chance. She swiped out with her claws again, catching him in the muzzle. The bear let out a quaking roar that shook the ground beneath them—far more intimidating than his bite. He whipped around and thundered toward her again. Out of the corner of her eye, she caught the glint of fangs from the other direction.

So, the assholes had started working together.

With the stream of water in her grasp, she slipped out of the black bear's path and slammed her paw to the ground. The water sprayed in all directions, a strong enough blast to disorient the bear, the wolf and the lion all skulking toward her. The other mountain lion paced back and forth as if he was waiting for the right opportunity to dive in. She wouldn't give him one.

The bear who had snarled at Sierra let out a howl in pain that echoed to the rafters of this place. The Red Rock alpha sank her teeth into his neck and wasn't letting go even as he thrashed. The other wolf rammed into her, but Sierra was an unstoppable force.

Navi didn't wait for the shifters to get their bearings.

She was a big enough panther to tower over them and she knew how lethal her strength could be.

Launching off on her front paws, she flew into the fray.

She rammed forward, the flat of her head slamming into the mountain lion's side. He swiped with his claws, but Navi turned around, heading for the next attack. The points of his claws nicked her tail, but she paid him no mind. The wolf found his bearings faster than the others and lunged for her, gray fangs bared. Once the tips of those fangs descended, Navi slammed her paws on the ground again with force. A stream of water rushed out to blast into him. He spluttered, crashing to the ground in a sloppy landing.

By the time the bear charged in her direction, she'd bared her fangs at the ready. He lumbered closer, closer.

Before she could sink her teeth into him, a blur caught her attention at the last moment. The other mountain lion rammed her in the side. Her side stung and she stumbled. The bear wasn't stopping. He rushed for her, his teeth glinting under the fluorescent light while he prepared to strike.

Navi rolled out of the way, back onto her paws before he crashed straight into her. She whipped around, but instead of taking a breath to recover, she claimed the offensive. Navi bounded off her front paws to vault towards the bear. She sank her claws in past his fur, digging her teeth deeper into his skin. Crimson flecks sprayed against the concrete floor as he roared.

She detached, landing on her feet as she circled around, the copper taste of blood on her tongue. A roar quaked from the basement of the warehouse, the sound jolting her with ice. Finn was fighting down there and she had no way of knowing how many he faced and if he'd survive. Every fiber of her being begged her to bolt in his direction and help. That was the bond speaking and she refused to indulge. He was a competent, trained fighter who she trusted.

Instead, she slammed her paws down, sending the pool of water beneath her spraying out toward her enemies. Under the fluorescent lights, the water glinted, blindingly so. She didn't wait for the droplets to descend—Navi rushed forward, ramming full force into the nearest mountain lion. Her head hit his side with a solid *thunk* and he went tumbling back.

Before he could recover, she whipped around, bounding for the wolf. Anxiousness burned within her, spurring her forward, faster.

Slash.

She raked her claws into the wolf's muzzle right when his jaws snapped open. A strangled sound somewhere between a howl and a whimper came from the bastard's throat. Navi didn't stop, pushing forward with another slice that coated her claws in hot blood, this one scoring his front haunches. The wolf whipped his head away, more scarlet flecks imprinting on the slate floors.

A loud howl came from where Sierra still fought against the wolf and the bear. She'd accumulated several scratches and a cut bled but, out of the three, the Red Rock alpha remained on top. The one wolf was missing an ear and the bear limped while it attempted to charge.

Teeth glinted under the overhead lights, drawing her attention. The mountain lion who'd been circling on the defensive struck.

Navi ducked, muscles tensed as he soared toward her, ready to descend. One problem with his straightforward attack, though. He wasn't fast enough.

She sprang forward, his neck on clear display as he tried to crash down upon her. As Tribe, she would always be faster. Navi sank her teeth into the meat of his throat and she jerked her head to the side, the wet tear of flesh resounding through the cavernous warehouse. The mountain lion tumbled to the ground, trying to loop around her for the door. Not like he could escape—Sierra had latched the door shut while in human form.

The three other attackers switched to defensive, their fur sticky with blood and tufts marring the ground along with the bloodstains. Navi paced in front of them, waiting for the next charge while her heartbeat pounded louder and louder in her ears. On the opposite side of the warehouse lay a desk against the far wall with stacks of paper on top. She'd be taking those with her when they made their escape.

Sierra lunged forward, snapping her jaws down on the other wolf's front leg with a crunch. Even as the fangs descended from the opponent, she ducked and used the weight of her movement and the tensile strength of her jaw to her advantage. The snap of the limb echoed to the rafters. The wolf howled with agony and blood dripped from Sierra's muzzle when she stepped away.

Navi marched back and forth before the shifters. The mountain lion near the door had sunk to the ground, losing blood faster than he could afford, while the other one prowled forward, and based on the twitch of his paw, he was ready to spring. The bear crouched low, those wounds keeping him from moving forward fast, and the wolf hid his damaged muzzle from view. Navi tensed, waiting for the attack of the other mountain lion.

Until she caught the acrid scent in the air, and turned her head to see the smoke pouring from the basement at an alarming rate.

Chapter Twenty-One

By the time they'd snuck to the back of the warehouse, Sierra and Navi had flung the door open and made their loud and flashy entrance. Jer slunk close behind Finn, brimming with a seriousness that he didn't often show. While Jer could give it as good as any shifter, he was always more of a lover and a thinker than a fighter, unlike Finn, who rolled on brawn. The second the girls announced their presence, he forced his wolf in place to keep from bolting up front to join them. The urge to protect was a fierce one to wrangle. But Sierra and Navi were two of the strongest fighters he'd met, and this was his one chance to go after Rossi.

He crept through the stacks they'd slunk around the night before, heading in the direction of the basement. Rossi hadn't been among the guys up front and chances were he'd be cooking the meth in the basement again. The scent here stripped his nostrils with the intensity of paint thinner and he wasn't relishing revisiting the disgusting stench in wolf form. The steps leading to the basement were coated in grime, as were the walls. Even the door had been left open a crack for further ventilation, since the jury-rigged vents they'd set up could only do so much.

"Why did I volunteer for this?" Jer grumbled, keeping close behind him.

"Because you love me," Finn responded with a smirk, taking the first step down. He paused, listening for any sound from below. The clank and rattle of whatever equipment they used masked the rustle of movement from whoever waited below. "If you spot any sort of paperwork down there, grab it," he murmured. "Navi needs intel on why Mackey has the Landsliders doing these drug and smuggling runs in the area."

"Does that mean I can lean back and watch while you fight all the big bads?" Jer responded, humor in his tone even though his voice skated to a near whisper.

Finn shook his head while he edged down the steps. "I'll do the heavy lifting." With each step closer, his heart pounded a bit faster and he couldn't help the rush of adrenaline through his veins. He didn't think he would get the chance, but, unlike yesterday, this time he wouldn't freeze. This time, he would deliver the sentence Dale Rossi deserved. He stepped to the door and almost gagged from the fumes filtering through the opening.

He was done creeping around. Finn didn't try to peer in the door or listen—he kicked the door wide open and strode inside.

The setup was even more of a mess than he'd expected, three once-white folding tables spread out against the walls and filled with a mess of bottles, carboys and tubing that teetered one step away from implosion. Paint peeled off the walls in large patches and debris and scorch marks decorated the concrete flooring. Liquid bubbled in the tubing and the steam traveled up to the ceiling, a couple of large fans directing it toward the vents. Two guys stood at the tables with their backs to him as they measured from the bottles in their hands. Their shoulders tensed upon his entrance, but neither dared to move until they'd finished pouring whatever caustic liquid they were messing around with.

The third bastard in the room was the very guy he'd come here for. *Dale Rossi.*

He'd recognize the sour face anywhere. Even though the man's eyes were red-rimmed now, probably from working with drugs his entire life, he had the same deadened look he'd always had. The man's brows furrowed in irritation, and Finn didn't miss the way the bastard's claws popped out. His stomach bottomed as he met Rossi's gaze, but he didn't step back. He would not falter.

"Long time no see," Finn said, not bothering to hide his fangs with his grim smile.

"Who the hell are you?" Rossi asked, stepping a pace away from the door. The man was a coward through and through — guaranteed he would be inching toward some sort of weapon.

Finn continued his approach, one slow step at a time. "You don't remember me? I'm hurt," he said, in a dry tone. "I'm the kid you left orphaned after you murdered my folks, the junkies who used to run for you." Jer crept behind him, sticking to the opposite wall while he made his own, quieter approach. At this point, the two guys who'd been working at the tables set their equipment down. They both pivoted around to see what was causing the ruckus.

Recognition flashed in the man's watery eyes and Rossi's scowl deepened. "Sounds like I did you a favor. If they're the wastes of space I remember, they sure as hell weren't much use as runners, let alone parents."

The growl ripped from Finn's throat unbidden.

He could still smell the metallic scent of the blood that had coated everything in the motel room, splatters across the mattresses, the paisley carpeting and the scratch-and-dent nightstand. His father had been lying on the floor, flaps of mottled skin on the ground and his chest shredded. His mom's throat had been torn out and she lay collapsed on the other side of the bed, her limbs askew. Then the door had creaked, Finn hid and Rossi and his guys sauntered back in with incriminating crimson painting their hands. They'd gone straight for the nightstand, grabbed the baggie of blow his folks had stashed and out they'd gone, as if they hadn't snuffed out two lives.

Finn's claws came out and he wasn't sure how long he could keep his wolf leashed.

"Doesn't matter," he responded, his voice filled with loathing. "That was never your call to make."

Rossi glanced to the door, as if he was figuring how fast he could alert the rest of his crew. Despite the way Ace had loomed in his memories, time had changed them both. Finn had grown taller, stronger and into the sort of fighter who could take on all three of these bastards while barely breaking a sweat.

"There's an intruder down here," Rossi called at the top of his lungs, the sound reverberating throughout the room.

Finn flexed his claws while the shift prickled beneath his skin. "They're not coming," he growled and the wolf emerged.

Silver and rust-red fur began forming in patches and his bones melded into those of a wolf as he transitioned. His shirt ripped in the process. A moment later, Finn shifted onto all fours and was facing the asshole who'd left him an orphan — and his wolf side didn't know the meaning of mercy.

The moment Finn began the transition, Rossi did as well and his two cronies followed suit. Within seconds, three wolves faced him, mangy, ratty creatures without any of the majesty of the Red Rocks he ran with. Finn didn't blink twice. Jer remained in human form, his gaze flicking to them while he edged around the corner of the room in the direction of the filing cabinets. They'd fought together a thousand times before and, in team formations, it often helped to have one in each form.

Finn paced in front of the door, waiting for the first wolf to strike.

Two of them leapt for him in unison. Rossi, the coward, hung back to watch.

Finn crouched low to the ground, preparing for their descent.

When their paws hit the ground, he darted past and whipped around to face them. By the time the first guy pivoted around his way, Finn hurled his full weight into the bastard. He barely noticed the sting of the slam, his blood pumping faster and faster. The wolf stumbled back a couple of paces, colliding with the other one, and Finn took ruthless advantage of the chaos. Finn snapped his jaw down on the closest leg and, when his teeth sank in, he yanked back. A piercing howl came from one wolf and the other rammed into his side.

The breath flew from him in a fierce sweep, but he let go of the limb and turned to face the opposite opponent, blood and spittle dripping from his muzzle. Finn crouched on his back legs before launching himself forward at top speed. The wolf had barely settled on his back paws when Finn collided with him, the force propelling them against the wall with a crunch.

In his peripheral, Finn caught Rossi padding toward the door. *No fucking way.*

He bolted toward Rossi at full speed. Before the scumbag could make a break for the door, Finn landed in front of him, fangs bared. Rossi let out a growl, lunging forward, but Finn didn't back down or step out of the doorway. Even as those teeth snapped in front of him, Finn dipped right beneath to slam his head into Rossi's windpipe.

"Watch out." Jer's voice broke through the resounding growls and the bubble and clank of the meth production.

Except, before Finn could turn around, Rossi snapped at him again, this time sinking his teeth into his shoulder. He shrugged off the sting, and a growl ripped from his mouth. Finn lashed to the side, trying to thrash out of the grip. He only got resistance, those points sinking in deeper until his muscles started to scream in pain. Finn gritted his teeth and pushed forward instead, the sudden movement breaking his vise grip.

Right in time for the other wolf to ram headfirst into him.

Pain seared his side as he stumbled back, the force sending him colliding with Rossi.

"Out of the way," Jer shouted again. Finn didn't know what his packmate planned, he just knew he didn't want to be crouching where he was when it happened. Finn lunged for the entrance, blocking the way so Rossi couldn't slip past.

A second later, one of the beakers hit the floor next to the wolf who'd attacked. Frantic howls resounded through the tight space a second later as sizzling followed, and whatever fluid had been in the container began eating through the beast's flesh, increasing the burnt, horrible stench in this room.

"I've got the other one," Jer called. "You handle Rossi."

Finn settled in the middle of the doorframe, staring down Dale fucking Rossi, the sleazebag who'd done more damage to this area than most accomplished in a lifetime. *Some goddamn wolf.* The man had no honor, no pride and had only survived this long by selling out everyone he could. The biggest mistake he had made was returning to Red Rock territory where a broken kid had become one mean motherfucker who wouldn't allow scum like that to thrive.

In an instant, the shadow that had loomed over him for so long dissipated. He saw the craven wolf who stood quaking before him and he knew deep in his marrow he could take him down.

Rossi crouched, ready to take any opportunity to dart past him and escape, his eyes watery and weak even in this form. Finn wouldn't give him the option.

Finn feinted forward and the asshole fell for it. The moment he faked his leap, Rossi bolted for the door. Finn whipped around to slam into him full force, sending him sliding across the concrete, his claws screeching with the movement.

Except, he wouldn't get the chance to rise.

Finn crashed into him and buried his fangs in the monster's neck.

Rossi thrashed, but Finn was far heavier and pinned him with his front paws, clamping his jaw like a vise around the wolf's throat.

He might never get the chance to change his parents' future, but one thing had become clearer than ever since Navi had rolled into town.

Finn could change his own.

He tightened his bite and yanked back, the muscle tearing with the motion. As his jaw clenched down even more, an audible crack sounded, the force reverberating through his fangs. Blood spurted from the massive tear in Rossi's neck and the wolf went limp in his grip.

Finn let go, blood thick on his tongue, the liquid dripping from his muzzle. Rossi dropped, slumping on the ground, his form still. Finn crouched, sniffing around him and watching to see if his chest moved. But no ragged breaths shuddered, no feeble wisps. Those pale eyes were glazed and still in death.

He sucked in a sharp breath. A triumphant adrenaline rush surged through him, but even while he felt the kick of satisfaction, he knew in his heart killing Dale Rossi wouldn't erase his complicated past. His parents were dead and his past still filled with pain. But resolution settled in his gut. Now he knew this was what he wanted in life—tracking down bastards just like Rossi who had escaped justice for too long and making them pay for their crimes. He was made for this.

A shout came from Jer, drawing Finn's attention.

His best friend backed against the table when the wolf he'd burned with acid lunged for him.

When the table shook, several of the beakers and jars on the table toppled over. Liquids spilled across the surface, mingling with one another and seeping into the seams, underneath the carboys and tubes. The sound of shattering glass echoed through the room.

Jer threw himself forward out of the way right as the wolf went sailing to crash into the table.

Oh, hell.

Finn's ears began to ring right as the blinding light flashed in front of him and, for a moment, the world went blank while the lab exploded.

Thick, oily clouds poured out in every direction and even as Finn took a couple of gasps in, he spluttered out. Jer was farther in there. He needed to get to his friend. Unable to see much more than the choking tufts, he padded one careful step at a time. Heat crackled around him, singeing his fur, and amidst all the noxious clouds, he caught the glimmer of flames. This room would burn up within minutes.

He thudded against something solid and he dipped his muzzle down. Not like he could smell or see anything around him. Fingers wove through his fur, which had grown crispy around the edges.

Jer's grip tightened in his fur and Finn led them forward. He might not be able to see, might not be able to sense anything amidst the fumes searing his nostrils and the tendrils of flame biting at his paws, but he would follow the airflow to the open door.

Finn needed to make it out of here and back to Navi. He refused to accept the alternative.

Chapter Twenty-Two

The moment the explosion rocked the building, Navi's heart almost stopped.

Finn was down there. She had to get to him.

Even though the mountain lion was preparing to lunge, Navi didn't give a damn. She bolted toward the back of the warehouse, tearing across the linoleum. Fear flushed through her body in one deadening sweep. She'd just found her mate. She couldn't lose him now.

The breezes rifled through her fur as she soared past the stacks, racing through this massive warehouse at breakneck speed. If the meth lab had exploded, they'd be lucky to find any survivors. Cold sweat prickled over her. Hell, forget survivors below—they'd all be lucky to escape the inferno to follow.

Navi skidded to a halt in front of the staircase leading to the basement. She squinted, her eyes burning in the wake of the smoke that roiled out from the open door. Yet no one emerged. Protocol would have her getting

Sierra, unlatching the front door and making her escape with the papers in this place before it went up in flames.

Protocol be damned.

She summoned her power, drawing the water from the earth to pool at her feet. Navi focused all her will into the motion, ignoring the roiling smoke and the insistent beat of fear ramming into her. Once she'd gathered pools of water, she stepped down the stairs, sending trickles ahead of her, hoping and praying they'd combat the fire, not do worse damage.

She padded down the steps, the gusts of heat drying out her fur with every step closer. Even though she couldn't see much beyond the choking gusts, flames flickered, ones that would spread in a heartbeat.

The clouds in front of her moved. Navi squinted, trying to make out the figure in front of her, if friend or foe emerged.

A wolf she'd recognize anywhere stepped through the doorway. *Finn.*

Navi stamped her foot on the ground, her heart squeezing so tight with relief it could burst. Jer stumbled out right behind him, clutching the doorframe as his chest rattled with coughs. Navi caught her mate's gaze and nodded toward the front of the warehouse. They'd have time for reunions later. Right now, they needed to get the hell out of this burning building.

Finn loped up the steps, halting every time he huffed from the smoke and chemicals he must've inhaled. Jer followed close behind and Navi took the lead, making sure to keep her pace measured so she didn't lose track of them.

They'd reached the top of the basement steps when another boom quaked the meth lab.

Flames licked the timbers of the doorframe and traveled up the steps.

Finn surged forward, faster, and Jeremiah kept up as best he could on two legs. Despite the need to rush itching Navi's hind legs, she waited until they'd taken off across the warehouse and followed in the rear. The heat from the flames prickled her skin and if they waited around any longer, they'd be trapped in this warehouse while it burnt to the ground. The first creaks and groans began of beams from below while the flames licked them up.

Navi surged along with the other two and they booked it across the warehouse.

When they emerged past the stacks to the front where she'd left the other Landsliders, the front door was swinging open, and Sierra was the only one remaining, shifted to her human form. The alpha was grabbing any stacks of paper she could, but she whirled around when they burst into view. Once she caught sight of them, Sierra gripped the papers she had in her hand and abandoned the task, breaking into a run toward the front door.

Finn's ragged breaths troubled her and Jeremiah suffered the same, coughs exploding from him even as they kept pace. Not like any of that would matter if they didn't escape in time.

Sierra had reached the front door by the time they closed in on it and Navi wasn't stopping for anything. The creaks and groans from the back of the warehouse increased and, when she paused to glance back, the amount of noxious smoke through the place had tripled within seconds, spreading in their direction. Finn and Jeremiah followed Sierra out through the exit and Navi came out last, nudging the door shut behind her with a slam.

The cooler night air hit her lungs and her chest throbbed as she wheezed in response. The moment they made it near the perimeter of the warehouse, Finn hacked up crud onto the gravel and Jeremiah bent over and began hurling. She could barely smell anything and her throat felt coated, like she'd swallowed acid for the last hour. Her fur was singed and the skin beneath tender.

Navi shifted into human form, the transition slower than normal. On top of her depleted energy from tapping into her powers, the aftermath of the explosion had left her sore. As her fur changed to skin and she shifted onto two feet, her injuries throbbed and patches of her skin were sensitive from the heat. Even with the accelerated healing powers of her kind, she'd ignored the gouges she'd received in there during her fight, and Finn would take even longer to heal.

She hadn't made it a few paces toward the Challenger before hands wrapped around her. Navi was too exhausted for a fast reaction time, but she didn't need to worry—she knew who held her tight. Finn's chest pressed against her back and, despite the way her skin ached, she sank into his embrace, the relief soaking through her.

Navi turned around to face him and her eyes heated at the sight of her mate standing in front of her. She traveled her fingers across his skin before she could help it while she examined him for injuries. He'd sustained some intense burns along his arms, along his back, and a couple of areas leaked blood. She'd bandage him up when they got out of here, but first she needed to place a call to the emergency services again. The firefighters would have a field day with this one.

Finn circled his arms around her and drew her tight to him. She didn't wait for him and pressed her mouth to his, just as anxious to feel his touch in the wake of the battle they'd fought. She could barely taste him or even feel his lips with how raw her skin was, but the simple act sent shuddering relief through her.

This was what she'd been terrified of, what Akio dealt with every time his wife joined him on a mission. As much as the explosion had struck her dumb with fear, she trusted Finn to fight by her side. If they'd weathered this, she had faith they could brave the challenges they would face on the road. As she stared into those tender eyes she'd come to know so well, she saw a future so beautiful it made her heart break.

Sierra approached, dropping the stack of papers on top of the Challenger in front of them. "Between letting those slimy bastards run free and getting cues on what Kendricks might be up to, I chose the latter. I hope there's something in here you can use."

Navi shook her head, breaking away from Finn to grab the stack of papers. "You made the right call. Not like I expected any less from a Red Rock." She glanced to Sierra, Finn and Jeremiah who gathered around the car while the warehouse crackled and blazed in the background. "I've traveled through many, many cities and I can honestly say I've never met a pack like this. You're a remarkable crowd."

Her eyes locked with Finn's. She'd traveled all across the East Coast on Tribe business, but those words held true when it came to him. Navi had had one-night stands, friendships and even attempts at relationships crumble to pieces. As Tribe, she was never able to sustain anything lasting. However, for the first time in her life, she allowed herself to hope again. Because all those mistakes, all those failed relationships didn't hold a candle to the connection that blazed stronger than the fires in the distance between her and Finn.

They could hop from state to state, from one hotel to another, but the distance no longer mattered, because Navi had found her home.

Chapter Twenty-Three

Finn pulled in front of the Beaver Tavern, his nerves on edge.

A hand rested over his, the comforting touch the only thing he'd ever need. He glanced over to his mate, Navi, who leaned back in the seat as if she belonged there. The sight of her made him want to make a detour before the rendezvous with Jess and the others a couple of hours north. Several weeks had passed since he'd killed Dale Rossi and they'd broken up the smuggling ring, and he'd healed well despite a painful first week. Except, despite the way they'd taken down the head distributor, Mackey's involvement remained complicated.

Because Joe Ganzorig's name was stamped all over those invoices. And when they'd driven down to pay their shaman friend a visit, his place had been cleared out. All those years Rossi had spent selling people out had caught up to him, because Ganzorig had made him into the scapegoat this time.

"Hey, we'll probably be around these parts before you know it," Navi said, her words bolstering him. "After all, something about this area seems to keep attracting Mackey's attention."

He swallowed, his throat tightening on reflex. He was shit at goodbyes and this would be the biggest one he'd ever faced. Today, he would say goodbye to the place that had nurtured him, one that helped him grow into the man he'd become. He would be leaving behind the gym he'd put up for sale, and lifelong friends who meant the world to him.

However, his wolf had stopped the restless march in his chest that had filled him with anxiety the past couple of years. His newfound path gave him the contentment he'd been longing for, the challenge he'd been searching for ever since he'd lost the alpha position. And he'd be fighting alongside a mate he not only adored but respected.

Finn sucked in a deep breath. *Game time.*

He hopped out of his driver's seat and headed for the front of Beaver Tavern. Navi slunk up behind him and, as they approached, she grew quiet with a contemplative look in her eyes. He stepped to the door, but the normal buzz and chatter wasn't flowing from inside.

The moment he stepped in, he understood why.

"Surprise!" dozens of voices hollered when the lights flicked on. Red Rocks of all ages, from the elders to the littles to his best friends, lined the tavern. Even Raven stood behind the taps as usual, a half-smile on her face.

A wide grin rolled onto his face and Navi smirked beside him, unruffled.

"You knew," he accused.

She shrugged. "Unlike you, I've got a poker face."

He shook his head, stepping inside as Sierra and Jer approached to greet him. Jer slung an arm around him and Sierra passed him a pint of Guinness.

Jer squeezed his shoulders and leaned his head in. He was Finn's oldest friend and, no matter how far he traveled, nothing would change that. "Should've known you wouldn't settle for the little leagues. Can't just aim for another pack—you've got to go and start working for the Tribe."

A sarcastic quip leapt to his lips, but he stopped himself. That fit their usual interchange, but he was leaving. "And you deserve to find your own happiness, brother." Their eyes met and, for a moment, he saw all the shattered pieces in Jer's gaze, one that gripped him, Jer and Raven alike. He'd fought to break the cycle, but it hadn't been easy. He hoped with all his heart that his friends had managed to do the same.

"Hard to believe our pack beta is leaving us," Sierra murmured, unable to hide the sadness in her voice. Finn swallowed the ale, and he couldn't dodge the way his eyes pricked with heat. "Your position might be filled, but you know, Finn Kelly, you'll never be replaced. You will always be a Red Rock."

"Always," he said, his voice coming out hoarse with emotion. That was the solemn truth, one it took finding the woman of his dreams and the adventure of a lifetime to learn. No matter how far he traveled, he would always be part of this pack.

Want to see more from this author? Here's a taster for you to enjoy!

Tribal Spirits: Forged Contracts
Katherine McIntyre

Excerpt

A month had passed since Finn Kelly had left, and with every day that passed, Raven's composure unraveled a little further.

Her grip tightened on the wet rag as she slid it over the chestnut surface of the bar, cleaning the sticky spilled beer and the rings left from the bottles. The dusky afternoon light spilled through the windows of their haven, Beaver Tavern, which had divots in the floorboards and a lingering scent of cedar that reminded her of home. Already, old man Gene had wandered inside and was nursing a pint at his usual spot, and a couple of the younger guys in the pack were arguing back and forth over their burgers.

Everything remained the same as normal, and yet her entire world had grayed around the edges. She'd moored her anchor to the wrong ship and wasted close to a decade distracting herself with the wrong guy. And no matter how much Sierra offered to spar with her and Jer made excuses to swing over to watch a flick or crack stupid jokes, they couldn't stop the way her chest throbbed, or how her skin itched so badly she wanted to tear it off.

Raven wasn't an idiot. She'd always known Finn Kelly wasn't in love with her, but he'd been the closest thing to feeling safe. When he'd driven off in his Challenger with his mate at his side and left the pack behind, he'd shattered that comfort. Now the lengthy shadows set her on edge, and each night when she returned to her empty apartment, her adrenaline spiked with every creak and groan of the old timbers.

So, she'd spent more time behind the bar, picking up as many shifts as she could, if only to drown out the memories she'd locked away ten years ago. Ones that crept closer with each passing day, threatening to drag her under.

Raven dropped the rag underneath the counter and straightened her ponytail, which had begun to slump in the hour she'd been here. She couldn't stop moving if she wanted to, amped up in a constant state of vigilance that wore her wolf to the bone.

The door to Beaver Tavern creaked when it opened again.

Jer stepped inside, his presence commanding her attention the same as always. *Not like anyone could help but get swept up by the sight of him.* The man's looks caused the air to vanish from the room and his sexual magnetism made her whole body flush with a single glance.

He caught her gaze and a heartbreaker smile rose to his lips, enhancing dimples that made her heart speed up every time. His clever eyes danced and his eyebrows tilted with a wicked edge, inspiring lust from just about every girl who crossed his path. He skimmed a hand through his tousled chestnut locks with an effortless grace as he sauntered in her direction. Based on the way her body reacted every time he entered the room, she should've been chasing after Jer all these years.

Except, with Finn, she'd felt safe. She'd been able to mute the turbulence storming within her, even if only for a little while.

Jer was another story.

His presence ripped her wide open and forced her to feel with such a strength she gasped for breath. She couldn't hide or escape from the constant pulse of surrender, surrender, surrender. Raven would never be able to take the risk. For her, the options narrowed down to fight or die, and the fight for her own mind never ended — not after the past she kept secret to this day.

Besides, even though Jer managed to conceal his pain behind so many easy smiles, the hurt ripped into her as if it were her own. He fought his own daily battle — they both did. And with the stormy seas buffeting the two of them around all these years, she could barely believe they hadn't drowned. Anything more than friendship might sentence them both.

"Have you been getting any sleep?" Jer asked, flattening his palms on the surface of the bar. Concern ringed his tone, concern she didn't want to face.

"More than you, stud," she responded with a sharp smile. "Though don't take that as an invitation to go into the tawdry details of your latest conquests. I've heard more than I ever wanted to know from the other pack females."

He shook his head, a half-smile on his face as he took a seat. "Talk is cheap. You know if you ever want to verify for yourself, all you have to do is ask." He said it with smooth perfection, a delivery that would make most girls squeeze their thighs tight. Except Raven had the stupid curse of soaking in emotions like a wet sponge, and his offer wasn't brimming with heat. The wave of hopelessness crashing off him slammed into her.

The guys might tease Jer for his distractions, but most of them egged him on, half in awe of his prowess. Not many people understood how he'd withered away over the years, losing himself in the chase, the same way Raven had thrown herself into Finn. She'd recognized his damage early on, a mirror to her own, and if they ever collided, they'd rip each other open until nothing remained.

Raven grabbed a pint glass from the stack and began filling it with the porter he drank on the regular. She placed the beer in front of him. "Keep on wishing, babe," she purred. "I'm STD free and want to remain that way."

She wielded her tongue like a whip because she valued Jer too much to become another distraction for him, another notch on his bedpost. And after Finn had left their damaged trio, the two of them had fought to stay afloat against the rising tides. He shook his head, the smile clinging to his face even though his eyes didn't reflect it back.

He lifted the pint to his lips and swigged with an unsettling quickness. She hadn't been the only one off as of late, but whatever had changed with Jer, he remained tight-lipped on the subject.

Ever since the East Coast Tribe had left the area, quiet had returned, since the powerful shifter governing force tended to set garden-variety shifters on edge. However, it wasn't the peaceable serenity that arrived with the cool autumn breezes. The pebbling chill in the air promised trouble, no matter how hard she tried to convince herself otherwise.

"How are the new responsibilities?" Raven asked, picking up the rag and continuing to polish the same gleaming spot, over and over.

"Finn left some pretty big shoes to fill as Sierra's beta." Jer placed the glass onto the counter and slumped forward. "She's encouraging as anything, but she holds back around me. Finn knew how to push through that shit — the bastard was so thickheaded he'd ram right through most folks' hesitations. I don't operate his way."

"So, what you're saying is it's an adjustment." Raven couldn't help her wan smile at the sight of him there, fingers raking through his curls, exasperated. That was the Jer she'd first met, a sweeter one who felt more than he'd ever admit. Those glimpses were worth the slight distance she kept between them, how she'd never succumbed to the temptation to slip into his bed. And Spirits above, there had been so, so many times she'd wanted to over the years.

"Give me contracts and arbitrations with pack disagreements any day over this beta nonsense. At least I make bank doing that business, and I'm arguing already presented cases. Beta business means having an opinion of my own and standing behind it, all the shit Finn and Sierra get their rocks off on."

Raven would be lying if every mention of Finn's name didn't make her wince, but she kept her mask in place, same as she'd been doing for years.

The door to Beaver Tavern creaked open. The scent drew her attention at once, and her wolf perked to attention. Not pack.

Not pack, but familiar, in the worst sort of way.

Christian Denzel strode into Beaver Tavern with a smirk on his lips and the devil in his gaze. He hadn't changed in over a decade, with the same sweep of dark hair and even darker eyes against alabaster-pale skin. The moment Raven caught sight of him, the pint glass she was preparing to stack almost slipped from her grasp. Out of the ghosts to appear from her past, only one would be worse than him.

His coyote scent attracted attention as folks looked up from their tables when he walked by. But he didn't pay them any mind. His gaze branded her, and she couldn't tear hers away. Most of the time, she was safe behind the bar at Beaver Tavern, as if it created a barrier between her and the rest of the world. However, right then she was chained there when her wolf lunged in her chest, begging to run, run, run, anywhere but this place.

The squeak of Jer's chair when he faced the intruder snapped her to attention.

"If you're looking to stir up trouble, you stepped into the wrong bar," Jer said, lifting his pint. Even though he gave him a lazy glance, only a fool would trifle with their pack lawyer. He was sharper and smarter than almost any other Red Rock.

"Me? Trouble?" Christian said in mock surprise as he took a seat. His gaze fixed on her with a steadiness that carved right underneath her skin. "I'm here to relay some news, and maybe catch a drink with an old friend."

Raven swallowed hard. *No.* The past lay behind her, one she hadn't brought along when she'd joined the Red Rocks. Her insides chilled colder than the ale in the taps. Jer glanced to her then Christian, his eyebrows furrowing in response. She needed to defuse this situation now, before Christian went running his mouth and ruined everything she'd built there.

"What can I get for you?" she asked, her voice coming out like battery acid. If she'd had liquid silver on hand, she'd dump it straight into a pint glass and force it down his throat. Christian's face was one of the ones she'd buried from memory, and his sleazy tone one that whispered in her mind when she tried to settle for bed. The brand on her hip felt as if it burned from the phantom sensation of past regrets.

A grin rolled to Christian's lips while he leaned forward at the bar. "I'll take a pint, darling. You look like you've been doing well for yourself."

Raven poured a pint of their cheapest ale and shoved it forward, foam sloshing over the edges. Christian's expression never changed, mocking amusement gleaming in his eyes. Unlike the teenager she'd known back then with his flannels and jeans, he now wore a suit, giving him a city-slicker vibe that married so well with his sleazy personality.

"Where do you two know each other from?" Jer asked, glancing between them. Raven tensed, and Christian's laugh scraped against her nerves. The gazes from the other patrons in the bar prickled along her skin, an awareness she couldn't shake no matter how hard she tried.

Before she could make up some lie, Christian interjected. "We ran around in the same circles in our youth, but I haven't seen this one in years. Almost like she's been avoiding us."

Raven's grip tightened on the rag she held, and her claws pricked out. "Maybe because the lot of you were assholes. Drink your beer and get the hell out, Christian." Her words came out low, but they seethed with intent.

He took a sip from his pint before unleashing another grin. This one glittered with the insidious intent she'd expected from the start. "Hey now, I showed up for a reason. Figured the Red Rock Pack should get *some* notice."

"Notice about what?" Jer had been paying attention, but it was clear this commanded his full focus.

"I've been hired to represent the Coalition of Human Rights. As much as they dislike our kind, they needed a shifter on the inside to handle the bigger problem, because what they detest even more are the pack formations and the Tribes themselves. Collections of shifters are a threat to humanity," he recited, as if he'd been practicing the speech in front of the mirror.

"Selling out your own kind?" Raven interjected. "Color me surprised."

"I haven't seen you working around these circles before, and I know most of the other lawyers in the region. Who's your employer?" Jer asked, tapping his fingers along the surface of the bar.

Christian's grin widened. "I work for Hansen Associates in Philadelphia. A bit of a distance from the hick central I grew up in."

"And what does the Coalition want?" Jer asked, his voice the sort of calm promising imminent explosion. "We keep to ourselves, and our relations with the local humans have been nothing but friendly."

"Oh, didn't you hear?" Christian said, with the assured smile they wouldn't have heard whatever filth he prepared to expound. Raven needed to retract her claws, but the instinct thrummed inside. Her wolf was covered in so many scars that she lashed out, begging her to shift and thrash this bastard.

Christian plucked out the folder he'd been carrying and placed it on the bar counter. Raven didn't trust herself to look at it, but Jer's expression darkened the moment he scanned the papers. A low growl thrummed from their new pack beta, and at once, every single Red Rock in the bar turned their way.

She sucked in a shaky breath and glanced down.

'Petition for Sale of Ricketts Glenn State Park.'

The ground slipped from beneath her. "That's our territory." The words rolled out even as the numbness filtered through her veins. Even though Red Rock owned portions outside of the state park that couldn't be touched, when it came to pack demarcations, everyone understood that her pack claimed the rest of it as well.

Christian smirked. "Except, as of late, the state's been behind on payments. The Coalition of Human Rights knows how dangerous these packs congregating can be. Their plan is to buy out the land, and, honestly," he paused to cast a cursory glance around the bar, "if this is all the Red Rock pack is pulling in, I doubt you'll be able to outbid them."

Raven couldn't help herself. Her fist went flying right toward the smarmy bastard's face.

Christian's hand shot up to catch it. Her knuckles thudded against his callused palm. No matter how he might play pretend at being genteel, the man was the sort of dangerous bred from the worst places. The chestnut bar dug into her hips while she strained at the seams to keep from shifting. Jer cast a worried look her way before he snagged the folder from the surface of the counter top.

"Temper, temper, Tigerlily," Christian murmured, igniting the flames inside her all over again. That nickname. She'd last heard it on *those* lips. Raven was going to be sick.

She stepped back a pace, her claws slipping out and fur beginning to prickle along her skin as if she was a kid again who couldn't control her shift.

"What's going on here?" a commanding voice rang out from the door. In the frame stood the woman who'd kept the pack together, the one who would fight intruders tooth and claw to protect their territory. Sierra Kanoska had arrived.

Home of Erotic Romance

Sign up for our newsletter and find out about all our romance book releases, eBook sales and promotions, sneak peeks and FREE romance books!

About the Author

Strong women. Strong words.

Katherine McIntyre is a feisty chick with a big attitude despite her short stature. She writes stories featuring snarky women, ragtag crews, and men with bad attitudes — high chance for a passionate speech thrown into the mix. As an eternal geek and tomboy who's always stepped to her own beat, she's made it her mission to write stories that represent the broad spectrum of people out there, from different cultures and races to all varieties of men and women. Easily distracted by cats and sugar.

Katherine loves to hear from readers. You can find her contact information, website details and author profile page at http://www.totallybound.com